BLOW A DEADLY KISS

Jonathan Paul Fagan

For my wife and daughters, thank you for all your encouragement.

PROLOGUE

"Two more hours, just two more hours," Tim Allwood thought to himself. He had recently booked a last-minute family trip to Florida with his family.

Susan, his work colleague, noticed his anxious demeanour. "Not long now Tim," she said laughing as they both served the customers.

Tim looked over. "Yeah I know, I'm just anxious to leave. We still have so much to do!" Susan smiled back. "You will be fine! You don't fly till Monday!"

The San Francisco National Bank was typically busy for a Saturday morning. The queue for the cash deposit register seemed never-ending. Tim glanced again at the huge bronze clock on the wall behind the bank's clientele, willing time to go faster.

At five to one Tim was relieved to see that the queue had finally dwindled to a few, so he took this opportunity to finally slam the TILL CLOSED sign on his register. Susan looked over at him. "What are your plans for the rest of the day then? Last minute packing I presume?" She asked.

"No, Emily has sorted all that out. I'm off to meet her and Beth for lunch." Tim said, picking up his suede overcoat and briefcase.

"So much for you saying you still have so much to do!

How is little Beth? Is she excited?" Susan chuckled.

"Oh, for sure. Every morning for the last 2 weeks she's asked is it vacation time yet!" Tim said laughing. "Well I guess I will see you in a week then! Enjoy work" He said, throwing a cheeky wink at her as he walked by.

"Huh, thanks! Have fun, Tim." Susan replied, wishing it was her time to go home. She glanced at the Bronze clock on the wall. "three hours to go." she sighed to herself, waiting for the next customer.

Half an hour later, Susan was checking if she had enough cash in her register when she noticed a familiar figure walk, almost drunkenly, into the bank. Susan sat at her desk, watching, as Tim walked across the large gold and cream coloured squared marble floor up to her register.

"Tim? What are you doing back here? She asked, frowning.

"My- my money. I want my money." Tim said, placing his card on the till in front of him.

"But- What- What's happened? I thought you were meeting Emily and Beth?" Susan asked, confused.

"My money. I want my money." Tim repeated, this time with a hint of aggression in his voice.

"Okay Tim," Susan said as she picked up his card and keyed in the details on her computer screen. "how much?" she asked with a concerned look on her face.
She managed to catch the eye of the bank manager, who was walking by with a potentially important client.

"How much do you want Tim? She repeated as she looked back at Tim. She noticed his eyes seem glazed over and unfocused. Almost empty.

"All of it. Give me all of it" Tim replied.

Susan began to ask "Tim, are you su-"

"All of it! Now!" Tim interrupted, his voice growing higher with each word, sweat beads beginning to appear on his forehead.

Looking over at the bank manager to see if he heard Tim's raised voice, which he did, Susan began to empty her cash till to give Tim his money.

"Tim, I don't have enough cash here!"

Tim began breathing rapidly. "Just- just give me the money!" slamming his fist on the grey metallic till.

Graham Howard, the bank manager, speed walked over to the commotion. "What the hell is going on here?! I am just finishing off a very important meeting! Tim! Why are you raising your voice?! You know better than that!"

Tim turned to Graham and mumbled something incoherent. "Tim? What's the matter with you? Are you drunk?" Graham asked, frowning, anger being replaced by confusion. Tim turned to the Bank's glass main doors and walked towards them.

Susan rushed round to Graham and quickly explained that Tim had left to go on vacation and shouldn't even be here. Both followed Tim out of the bank's main doors to see which direction Tim would take. Susan say's to Graham she will call Tim's home to speak to his wife and ask her about it. As they exit the bank, they saw Tim standing still, looking straight ahead. Graham approached him at his side cautiously to speak to him.

"Tim? Tim, are you-"

Within a split second, Tim reached into his inner jacket pocket and pulled out a gun.

As his wife and daughter walked down the street towards the bank to see where Tim is and why he hadn't shown up at the restaurant, they watch him pull out a pistol and place it to his temple and pull the trigger.

Half of Tim's head exploded as the bullet pierced through his brain and out the other side, splattering blood and brain fragments on the sidewalk. The exiting bullet burst out of Tim's head and flew directly into Grahams forehead, killing him, before coming to a stop.

Susan vomits noisily as the two dead bodies slumped to the floor in front of her. Tim's wife and daughter start screaming, along with all the other witnesses.

CHAPTER 1

"Kelly... I'm so sorry..." Detective James Cross mumbled as he sat alone on the lounge floor in his ground level apartment at 3 in the morning, looking at the picture. He took another swig of whiskey which he held in his left hand. In his right hand is his service gun that he had been given from the precinct.

Through tear filled eyes, he was staring at the picture on the table in front of him that was taken 2 months before his world fell apart. In the picture there is a tall man with short dark blonde hair and a brunette, whose shoulder length hair fell naturally over her pretty face. His 6ft frame towering above her 5.4ft, he was standing behind his wife holding the bump on her belly, which would soon become part of their family. Everything had seemed so perfect in that moment. At 36 years of age he had it all. A good job, a beautiful wife and was expecting their first child.

It was all taken within seconds.

If only I didn't come back.

He took another large gulp from the whiskey bottle, which was now half empty. He looked at the gun in his right hand and considered for a moment about ending it all.

Ending the pain, ending the suffering.

Then he shook that thought away. Although he is in a

drunken state, he also knew that Kelly would be pissed at him for even considering the thought. He drunkenly placed the bottle, and the gun, down on the table next to the picture and struggled to stand up.

Once he was on his feet, he staggered down the darkened corridor to what would have been the baby's nursery. They never did find out the sex of the baby, preferring to keep it a surprise. They had decorated the nursery neutral yellow colours. He pushed the door open and as he peered in grief overtook him again. He crumpled to the floor apologising. James reached up to his collar and pulled out a gold pendant from his shirt. He rubbed the pendant between his thumb and forefinger.

"I'm sorry," He sobbed, raising his other hand, wiping away a fresh stream of tears.

The day had started as normal as any other.

James had woken up before Kelly and he crept out of bed and went to the kitchen to make a coffee for him and a tea for Kelly. Before she fell pregnant, it was usually Kelly's job at the weekend. As the kettle boiled, he paid a quick visit to the toilet. After the deed was done, he washed his hands then continued to set about the coffee and tea task.

Carrying the drinks, he nudged the bedroom door open with his knee and saw that Kelly had woken up and was sitting up in bed, waiting for him.

"Hey honey," Kelly said through a stifled yawn.

"Good morning princess," said James as he sat the cup of tea down next to Kelly's side of the bed. He leant over to kiss her forehead and placed his hand gently on her belly.

"How'd you both sleep?" James asked, although he felt he already knew the answer.

"Urgh" was Kelly's reply, pulling a face. "Not good! This

one kept me awake all night. Think it was having a rave in there."

James walked over to his side of the bed and climbed in. "Well you can try and have a sleep this afternoon before we go for dinner." he said placing a hand over hers.

"I had forgotten about that," Kelly said as she sipped her tea. "is there any chance we can go early evening though? Any later and I'll be up all-night juggling heartburn and this hyper thing!" she said as the baby started kicking again.

That afternoon, after they had once again been to the baby store to get one of the many last-minute things that Kelly kept remembering, they were getting ready to go for a date night together.

"I'm so glad we're doing this Kacie," said James as he was buttoning up his shirt. Kacie was a nickname he had given her immediately after they married, her initials being KC. Kelly walked up to him and kissed him on the lips. He had to bend down as to avoid her bump.

"Me too," Kelly said, "after this new Cross addition in a month or so we will hardly ever get to do anything like this," James stuck his bottom lip out and pulled a sad face, then smiled as he tucked his shirt into his pants. "I know, and I can't wait." he placed his hand lovingly on her bump. Kelly stepped back and looked at James, half-smiling. "Kacie, what's that look for?" he asked, suspiciously. He could tell she had something on her mind. Kelly took a deep breath, and said "Look, don't be mad-"

James walked up to her, reaching for her hands. "Kacie, I couldn't ever be mad at you but please tell me, what's wrong?" James asked, concern spread over his face.

Kelly let go of his hands and walked back to her set of drawers. "Well I saw something the other day..." she started *saying, turning to James but avoiding eye contact with him. "I saw something, and I could not leave it. Honey, you work so hard for us and you have been pulling extra hours in, just so we have enough for when our baby arrives. It cost a lot, but I had to get it for you, as a thank you." Kelly opened her drawer and pulled out a small box that was tucked away, hidden in the corner. She took a deep breath and handed it to him.*

James took his eyes from her and looked at the box in his hands. "Kelly, what is this?"

"Just open it, James."

He slowly opened the box from the from front, lifting the top up. He gasped when he saw the gold Celtic pendant and chain inside. "Kelly..."

"Do you like it?" Kelly asked, smiling.

"Like it? I love it! Thank you!" he said, wide eyed.

"Look at the back of it," Kelly smirked.

James picked up the pendant and turned it around in his hand. He gulped when he read the back of it.

'By your side, forever I vow to be, I swear with every piece of me. I will cross the deserts, and swim the oceans with you, this I promise to be true.'

James looked up at Kelly, eyes full of tears. "Your wedding vows." He mumbled. Kelly nodded as he went in for a loving hug. "I couldn't leave it in the shop when I saw it. And I know how much you loved my vow to you, so I had that engraved straight after. I was going to wait to give it to you, but I couldn't resist." She said as he held onto her.

"I absolutely love it. Thank you so much, Kelly." he said, releasing her from the hug and kissing her on the lips.

They were on their way to their favourite Italian, Cibo e Vino, which was just less than 1 km from their apartment. They were walking down the street holding hands, taking it slow as Kelly couldn't walk very fast. They walked along the florally decorated sidewalk and neared the pedestrian crossing, talking about; possible baby names (they still couldn't agree on one), what the future held with their new son or daughter and what other things they may have to buy before baby Cross makes an appearance.

James wore the new pendant and chain with pride. Suddenly, he stopped walking.

"James? What's wrong?" an out of breath Kelly asked.

"Hold on a moment sweetie, I just gotta check something," James said as he fished his wallet out of his pocket and opened it out. "dammit! I forgot to pick up my bank card! I took it out earlier and left it in the kitchen!"

Kelly, who looked tired and red in the face, "James come on! I'm not waddling all the way back now. I'll wait here, and you can run back!" she huffed.

James apologised and gave Kelly a quick peck on the cheek. "I'll be five minutes tops!" he said as he started jogging back, which soon slowed to a speed walk.

Kelly waited a few more minutes, shuffling from side to side, feeling more and more uncomfortable by the second. She looked back down the road and couldn't see any sign of James returning. Kelly turned and looked down the other side of the street and saw the designated restaurant, which was just across the road. She decided to send James a text.

James neared his ground floor apartment door and held out his key when his phone pinged. He entered the apartment and went straight to the kitchen to get his card. He checked his phone as he picked the card up.

Going over to the restaurant, need to sit down! You klutz! Love you x

Smiling to himself as he walked out closing the door, James made his way back to the restaurant.

Waiting at the pedestrian crossing, 2 cars on either side slowed down to allow Kelly to cross the 4-lane road. She started to walk, holding her bump, past the first car on one side that had loud music blaring out. Kelly neared the middle of the road. She continued walking past the second car on the other side of the road.

A third car, which did not stop, sped past the side of the second car, ploughing straight into Kelly, throwing her into the air as the car carried on regardless at full speed. At the end of the road it lost control and crashed into a building.

Speed walking down the sidewalk, James was looking forward to having something off the special's menu, when he heard a commotion from up ahead.

A terrible sense of dread suddenly washed over him.

Sprinting at full pace, he soon arrived at the crossing where he left Kelly. His whole world fell apart in that one instance. He saw a body lying on the road, her face covered in blood. He ran over to his wife, screaming.

The other car drivers and passengers had gotten out and were all gathering around, some in tears, others in shock. One was on the phone for an ambulance, even though it was way too late, and another on the phone to the police.

Stroking his lifeless wife's face. "Oh God Kelly I'm so sorry! Please wake up! Please!" He sobbed as he brushed her brown hair out of her face, which was matted with blood.

"What happened?! What happened?!" James demanded, looking desperately at the witnesses.

They explained that as she was crossing a speeding car hit her and lost control, pointing to the crashed car, which also had people gathered round it. James didn't take his eyes off Kelly. It was then that James noticed the blood patch around his wife's legs. His heart broke even more.

Within a matter of minutes, although it felt like an eternity, the whole area was surrounded by police and ambulances. The vision of his wife's lifeless body being zipped up in a body bag will never leave James. A paramedic approached James with a towel to wrap round him and was about to treat him for shock when a thought struck him.

"What about the driver?! The one who drove into..." he tried to say her name but found it impossible. Throughout the chaos he hadn't even thought about the crash down the street, all his attention focused solely on his deceased wife and unborn child. "They died instantly," the paramedic replied. "I'm sorry but that is all I can say for now"

It was the early hours of the morning when James received a phone call from his captain at the SFPD.

"Hello?" James answered, physically and mentally drained.

"James, its Captain Fisher. I am so sorry to hear about Kelly."

"I... I still don't know what happened captain."

"I have the report here, James."

James sat upright in his sofa and listened.

"Male driver. Female passenger. Both 22 years old. The drivers name was Sean Conner, his girlfriend Jennifer Reilly. Witnesses say they were seen at McCoy's Irish bar. There was also an empty bottle of vodka found in the passenger side of the car. The results that came back report they both were drinking."

"Drinking? Are you telling me my wife and baby were killed by a drunk driver, Cap?" James had snapped down the phone, his blood boiling by the second.

Captain Fisher sighed. "Yes James, I am. I'm so sorry. Take all the time you need to process all of this. I'm sure you want to be alone right now. I'll be in touch in a few days. Take care James."

For the next six weeks James had become a recluse. Only leaving the apartment for the funeral. James had written a eulogy, starting off with how he and Kelly had met on a night out, neither expecting to fall madly in love within weeks. Her coffin was carried out of the church out to Kelly's favourite song, Angel by Sarah Mclachlan. After the service he only stayed about an hour at the reception. Stopping off at the liquor shop on the way home.

He survived mainly on takeout food and alcohol. Some people would say that alcohol is the reason Kelly died. But James knew better. It wasn't alcohol. It was Sean Conner. He was the one who decided to go driving under the influence that afternoon. James had wished Sean hadn't died just so he can see justice done.

Clambering back onto his feet, James wiped his face and stumbled into his bedroom. Not bothering to undress, he fell on his bed and closed his eyes.

Kelly.

CHAPTER 2

RING RING

Darkness, then a blur.

RING RING

Now a headache, and with that the memories came racing back.

RING RING

James slowly opened his eyes, groaning as his eyelids opened.

RING RING

James painfully lifted his head and looked at the digital clock next to the phone on his bedside table.

1:47pm

RING RING

James considered for a moment to ignore it. The pull of sleep still present making that

even more tempting. But then the damn phone would continue to ring and pound inside James's head making his headache even worse.

Rubbing his eyes, James leant on one arm and lazily reached for the phone with his other. He placed the receiver to his ear. "Uh, hello?" he groggily answered.

A deep voice answers back. "James, its Captain Fisher... Did I just wake you?!"

AH SHIT!

"Uh... no sir," James lied, coughing quietly, clearing his

throat, trying to sound like he had been awake for hours. "no, you didn't",

"Don't lie to me James. Listen, something's happened and I need you to get down to the San Francisco National Bank as soon as."

James quickly sat up in bed, his headache intensifying as he did so. He slammed his eyes shut in pain.

"Seriously?! Can't someone else do it?"

Now it was Captain Fishers turn to lie. "I don't have any other detectives available. I need you on this."

Captain Fisher knew that James had shut himself off from the world and needed to come back to reality. He told himself that the next case that comes along he will give to James.

One just came along.

"Captain, I'm really not in the right frame of mind for this just yet. I'm sorry" James said, shaking his head.

"James, you need to get back to work. I know you've been through hell son, but it's been six weeks since the accident. You need to get out that apartment. Just go down to the scene and have a look."

"Sir, I really don't think it's a good idea..." James paused then closed his eyes. Really not ready to go back to work but knowing that he can't stay off forever, James opened his eyes and sighed loudly. "Fine. Okay Cap, I'll do it. What's the case?"

"Suicide and involuntary manslaughter"

James shook his head. "Thanks for giving me an easy one sir"

"No problem. Get down there quick as you can before the scene becomes contaminated with too many officers." Said Captain Fisher before hanging up.

By the time James had popped some pain killers, washed, dressed and arrived at the at the bank; the scene had been taped off, the bodies had been cordoned off from the public and the bank was full of police officers.

When he walked in many cops stopped in their tracks and stared at James, for they either knew him or had heard about the accident from other officers.

Unsure what to say to him, a cop built up the courage to walk up to James.

"Hello sir, we didn't know you were coming back on duty." The young officer said.

James gave an awkward half smile "Me neither... till 40 minutes ago."

The cop looked awkward himself now. "Oh right. Well I'll tell you what we know so far," the cop said as they walked around the inside of the bank, stopping at the open glass doors, just on front of the cordoned off bodies. "The suicide victim's name is Tim Allwood," gesturing with his hand to the body of Tim. "The other victim's name is Graham Howard, he is -was – the bank manager," says the officer, indicating to the other body. "Tim came into work like usual. Started at 8:30am and finished at 1pm. He was due to go on vacation leave today. He left to go and have lunch with his family but returned to the bank approximately 30 minutes later, appearing to be drunk. However, his wife says that Tim didn't drink. He walked up to Susan," the cop said, gesturing to a distraught, middle age blonde who was being treated by specialist cops.

"She worked with Tim this morning. Said that she didn't notice anything out of the ordinary about him till he came back around 1:30pm"

James nodded. "Okay, and then what?" he asked.

The cop continued "Tim came back, acting out of character. Demanding his money. He started sounding aggressive when Susan asked why he had come back. When he didn't get what he wanted, Graham", gesturing to Graham's body again, "came over, asked what was happening, then Tim walked out of the building. Graham walked up next to him outside and that's when Tim reached into his inside pocket and put a bullet through his head and into Graham, who was stood right next to him"

Detective James nodded and then asks. "Okay, and the weapon?"

"Already being dusted for any prints other than Tim's."

"Good work. What about his family? Are they being spoken to?"

"As we speak. Although his wife and daughter are in shock, which is understandable, given that he killed himself in front of them," the cop winced as he realised he had just mentioned the words "wife", "daughter" and "killed", unsure of how James would react to it.

James looked suddenly absent minded for a moment. *Kelly*.

James snapped out of his reverie, although his eyes were still glazed over.

"Err, okay... where was he meeting his family?"

"At a diner up the street from here."

"I want to see the banks security footage starting from this morning."

Minutes later Detective James Cross was in the security room at the side of the bank's grandeur foyer, sat with

2 other officers and the assistant bank manager. On two of the seven screens in front of them was the footage of several cameras; an outside one of the main doors of the bank, an inside one of the main doors, one of the foyer and more behind the bank reception and bank clerks.

They had the collected footage of Tim Allwood, entering the building and working behind the cash register. Fast forwarding the footage, they arrived at the time when Tim was leaving. Together they watched Tim grab his overcoat and briefcase and walk out through the foyer and out the main doors. The screen instantly switching to the exterior footage.

Tim walked out and momentarily stopped, put on his coat before turning right and walked down the sidewalk and out of view of the camera. James asked to fast forward again and stopped when Tim was slowly walking back towards the bank exactly 27 minutes later.

Detective Cross asked to pause and zoomed in on Tim's face, which was expressionless.

He hit play again and Tim walked towards the main doors and pushed them open. The interior footage now on the screens. Tim walked drunkenly slowly over to the cash register, where Susan was sat. The screen shown Tim and Susan talking, the conversation inaudible. James can see Tim becoming irritated as the time passed by. Graham comes into view and walked over to Tim. Then Tim walks out and both Graham and Susan follow. The screen switched again to the exterior camera. The footage shown Tim stop outside the bank, Graham walked up to him then Tim reached into his inner pocket. Before Graham could react, Tim had already placed it at the side of his head and pulls the trigger, instantly killing himself and Graham.

Detective James walked out of the bank's main doors and turned in the direction as Tim did, towards the diner he was due to meet his family.

James looked all around him as he walked. He noticed a traffic camera on the other side of the road. He reached into his back pocket and fished out a small pad of paper. Flipping the pages over till he got to a blank page, he started writing.

He continued walking further and passed several shops and a hotel, making note of any outside security cameras. Eventually he reached the diner.

Walking back towards the bank, the officer that approached him earlier walked up to him. "What's the plan?" the officer asked.

Detective James Cross handed him the list of Security camera locations and the relevant buildings. "I want the footage from these cameras within the time frame that Tim left the bank and returned. Also send me the bank footage as well please. Have them sent to me at the precinct as soon as. I'm going there now."

The officer took the list from Detective Cross.

"I will," the officer hesitated, "but shouldn't you talk to the witnesses first?" he asked, frowning.

"It looks like you all have it under control here. Good work." James replied. The truth was that James wasn't ready for this and needed to at least go to the comfort of his desk, if he couldn't go back home. The officer took the hint and nodded. James turned and headed towards his car.

In the car park of San Francisco Police Department Central District, Detective Cross gripped the wheel, squeezed his eyes shut and fought back tears. On his journey to the station, he had seen a woman who resembled a lot like Kelly, albeit with shorter hair. His heart skipped a beat when he saw her smiling face. As hard as he tried not to, the thoughts of what could have been began formulating in his mind. He pictured them as a family, going on days out to the park, with his son or daughter and Kelly by his side. In his mind he saw his child growing up. He would never get to feel the happiness they would have shared together as a family. All he would feel is loneliness. And bitterness.

A smartly dressed African American man, on the slightly overweight side, opened the main doors of the SFPD station and peered across the car park out at James. A lot of the officers secretly referred to him as "Uncle Phil", as he resembled the character from *The Fresh Prince*. As he walked down the steps that led up to the entrance and started walking over, James wiped his watery eyes and got out of the car.

The African American man acknowledged James as he walked up to him.

"James, thank you so much for this." he said.

James faked a smile and stuck his hand out to shake.

"Captain Fisher, no problem." Detective Cross said, trying to steel his voice.

The Captain of the SFPD gently smacked away James outstretched hand and went in for a bear hug. "I'm sorry for everything that happened James, and I apologise for lying to you about having no one to get on this case, but you needed to get out of that apartment. I was worried about you. No one has seen you since the funeral and you weren't answering the door when anyone came by. I thought that maybe if you had a case it may take your mind off it."

Captain Fisher released James from the hug, looking uncomfortable.

"I realise I may also be wrong. Forgive me."

Detective James looked at Captain Fisher and sighed.

"I... I understand why you did it, Cap. I just couldn't face anyone or anything." James's voice began trembling. "I just felt so helpless that I couldn't save her. I still do. If only-"

"James, it wasn't your fault." Captain Fisher interrupted.

James continued, choking back the tears "If only I had remembered my card to begin with, or at least walked Kelly over to the restaurant before I went back, Kelly and my baby would be here now."

Captain Fisher raised a hand and placed it on James' shoulder.

"And if only Sean Conner had driven in the other direction, or had left the bar 5 minutes later. Life is full of *"what if's"* and *"if only's"* James. It wasn't your fault. You can't keep doing this to yourself." Captain Fisher said, softly. He let go of James shoulder and looked at the ground. "Do you need more time?"

James closed his eyes and thought about what Kelly would want him to do. Would she want him wallowing in self-pity at home, contemplating suicide every night he drinks... or would she want him at work, fighting to get his life back on track?

Taking a deep breath, he said. "Thank you sir, but no. I need to get back to work. I know I need this. I know it isn't going to be easy for me, but I can't stay at home drinking and feeling sorry for myself anymore. I need to quit drinking and to try and sort my life out."

Captain Fisher looked up at James and exhaled a sigh

of relief. His risky move had paid off. "Good! That's really good!" Captain Fisher said, smiling. He then extended his hand for James to shake.

After they shook hands both turned to the SFPD doors and walked towards the building.

Once sat at his desk, James explained the situation down at the bank and that he requested the footage of the cameras to Captain Fisher, who was seated next to James.

Captain Fisher nodded. "It arrived just before you pulled up into the car park. I haven't seen any of it, but I have forwarded it to you."

"Really? That's some fast work."

"I know, I don't think they dare take their time given who the case detective is."

James leant forward and turned on his computer. It took a moment as it kicked in and warmed up. Automatically it went straight to the police log on. James keyed in his details and the screen refreshed to the desktop, a navy-blue background and the San Francisco Police Department logo in the bottom right corner of the screen, which is of a police badge with an Eagle in the centre, its wings expanded. The top half of the eagle golden and the bottom half bronze. Below the eagle is a wavy banner with the Spanish words *ORO EN PAZ FIERRO EN GUERRA,* which translates to *GOLD IN PEACE, IRON IN WAR.*

James found the files that Captain Fisher had sent and both Captain and Detective leant closer to the screen. They watched the bank footage first. Fast forwarding from the moment Tim started work and left at 1pm to when Tim came back to the bank and shot himself in the head killing himself and Graham. James pressed the pause button. Captain Fisher didn't wince at the footage.

Being a seasoned cop had conditioned him and desensitised him from such images.

James said that the other footage is from the direction Tim had walked on the way to meet his family at 1pm. The other camera's footage started as soon as James hit the play button.

The footage that comes up is of a hotel entrance, the building next to the bank. The footage is of the entrance and caught the back of Tim walking up the street, eventually walking off camera.

James clicked play again.

The next footage also caught Tim but from the front this time. He is smiling to himself as he walked, clearly looking forward to his vacation with his family, as he walked towards the camera, unaware he was being filmed.

The next video is of a jewellery store, which was right next to the diner where Tim was due to meet his family. This time it was pointing up the street again. It caught the back of Tim walking up the sidewalk, carrying his briefcase. He was about to walk off the top of the screen, only his legs were now visible, when he stopped. There were another pair of feet, standing in front of him. Stopping him.

James paused the footage and made a note of the time stamp.

13:12

James hit play again. People continued walking by, unaware what was happening. The footage carried on for a few more minutes, neither pair of feet moving, before Tim turned around and walked back into full view of the camera. James hit pause again and made a note of the time.

13:14

James noticed that Tim was no longer holding his briefcase. And that he was no longer smiling. Instead he wore a blank expression now. Slowly he walked back down the street. Whoever stopped Tim, had turned and disappeared from the top of the screen.

CHAPTER 3

"So what time are we meeting the others?" Eleanor Knight asked whilst leaning towards the mirror in her bedroom applying her eye makeup, her dyed black hair with purple streaks tied back, save for two bangs of hair hanging either side of her forehead. She was wearing a black blouse and a red chequered skirt. Ryan walked in from the en suite bathroom and sat on the edge of the bed behind Eleanor, he was wearing chinos and a dark blue short sleeved shirt.

"We said we'd meet at 6:00. The movie starts at 6:45." Ryan said while pulling his shoes on.

"Can't wait!" Eleanor said sarcastically "Next time I get to pick which movie we go to see! The only reason I agreed is because you said we can go for something to eat afterwards! That and I haven't seen Shannon for what seems like forever." She complained.

Ryan slipped on his other shoe and tied it. He stood up, walked up behind Eleanor and bent down to kiss her cheek.

"I love you," he said. Eleanor turned to look at him and kissed him on the lips.

"Love you too," she replied.

Ryan smiled cheekily at her. "When we get back tonight you think that we..." he said suggestively with a wink. Eleanor looked back into the mirror to apply her make up again.

"Depends on how bad the film is." She said stubbornly.

They were standing outside the movie theatre 50 minutes later.

"Think we should go and buy the tickets now?" Eleanor asks looking at the queue already forming.

"We'll wait a few more minutes," replied Ryan, looking at his watch. He looked up at Eleanor and goes to give her a quick kiss on the lips when they heard "HEY YOU GUUUYS" in the same style as Sloth from *The Goonies.*

Ryan looked to his right and saw Reece and Shannon walking towards them. Shannon was grimacing with embarrassment.

"Sorry for being a bit late!" Shannon said.

"No worries. What kept you"? asked Eleanor, hugging Shannon.

"What do you think kept us? It's the same every time we go out!" chuckled Reece as he fist bumps Ryan. Shannon looked shamefaced. Eleanor laughed "So what we doing then? Getting tickets now and going for a drink at the bar?" she asked.

"Yeah, we just want to get some candy from the store first. No way are we paying them theatre prices." Reece said.

"Good idea. Honey, do you want anything?" Ryan asked as they walked to the store which was next door to the movie theatre.

"Ummm, surprise me! I'm going to have a quick smoke now, so I'll wait outside." she said as she let go of Ryan's hand and fished her pack of cigarettes from her handbag.

"I'm going to see what there is. Otherwise you'll only

get what you like!" Shannon said to Reece as they walk into the store leaving Eleanor outside as she places a cigarette in her mouth and lights it.

Eleanor was halfway down her cigarette and she didn't see, or hear the figure approaching. She was taking a long drag when she heard a movement from behind her. She jumped in shock, dropped her cigarette and turned to face the figure.

A minute later, feeling scared and confused, Eleanor felt her body turn involuntarily. *HELP ME!* she yelled internally as her body started walking towards the store. Up ahead a uniformed cop was walking towards the store as well. The figure behind her turned and left the scene as soon as he noticed the cop.

The cop smiled politely as he let Eleanor pass and enter the store first. The cop followed, intent on buying a bag of potato chips to keep him going till the end of his shift. All Eleanor could do is what she was told to do. She felt like a passenger in her own body, unable to control or do anything other than watch the scene unfold before her.

"Aha you're here," Ryan said when he saw Eleanor walk in. "which of these do you prefer?" he asked holding up two packs of candy. "Eleanor?" he frowned when she didn't acknowledge him at all.

She must be buying more cigarettes, no need to ignore me though Ryan thought hurtfully to himself as he turned back to the others.

Every fibre in her body was telling her to stop as she walked slowly passed Shannon and Reece who were discussing what snacks to get for the movie. A young man was behind the register, he appeared to be around 17 years old and had a spotty face. He noticed Eleanor walk slowly towards him.

Not used to being around attractive women, the young man blushed immensely when she stopped and stared at him.

"Err, may I help you?" he managed to squeak out. To his surprise, she turned and started walking round the register, never taking her eyes off him. Feeling a strange sense of excitement, he stared at her when she eventually was right next to him.

His heart thumping. "Miss, you aren't supposed to on this side." he said, quietly.

Ryan looked over and noticed what is happening. "El, what *are* you doing?" he asked out loud, catching the attention of the cop, who looked up himself.

In a flash Eleanor grabbed the young man and spun him around, reached into her bag and grabbed a serrated blade. She raised it up to his throat pressed it against his jugular.

"EL, WHAT THE FUCK?!" Ryan screamed as the scene unfolded in front of him.

"Give me the money" Eleanor asked calmly. Tears instantly streamed down the young man's face, the shock of it all being too much, taking away any words. Beads of blood appeared where the blade was being pressed.

"Give me the money" Eleanor repeated.

The cop rushed towards the till aiming his pistol at Eleanor's head. "DROP THE WEAPON! DROP THE WEAPON NOW!" he shouted.

Oh my god! Please help me! I'm not doing this! Eleanor screamed silently in her head as the cop aimed his gun at her.

"Give me the money." she said calmly, unable to stop

her voice.

"MISS, DROP THE KNIFE NOW!" the cop shouted again.

Eleanor, moving only her eyes, looked at the cop, Ryan and Shannon and Reece. Shannon was in tears with her hands over her mouth and Reece was holding her back. Ryan was stood with his hands in the air, as though he thought that would in some way calm the situation. "Eleanor, honey, please drop the knife! Look at what the hell you're doing!" he said.

I'm sorry was all Eleanor could think as she tore the knife across the young man's throat, spraying blood as she pulled. The cop aimed and shot Eleanor in the centre of the head, killing her instantly, her body falling to the floor as the young man fell on top of the counter, dying. The screams that followed filled the store.

CHAPTER 4

Detective James Cross was sat at his desk, frustrated that the security camera footage had been inconclusive. Yes, something had happened to cause Tim to stop walking to the diner and turn back to the bank in the Jewellers footage, but it had not caught *what* happened. The witnesses' statements were proving fruitless, and the weapon had no prints on it other than Tim's. Detective Cross had requested more security camera footage from any available further up the street *past* the diner, but there were few and far between, and they too had been inconclusive. Leaning back in his chair, he rubbed his tired eyes. Deciding to go and get a coffee he stood up and made his way to the coffee machine on the opposite side of the Precinct. He nodded in acknowledgement to his fellow detectives and officers he walked by, appreciating that they must have agreed amongst themselves to give him some space and not hound him with condolences.

He wasn't ready for that just yet.

He pressed his coffee preference on the machine and as he stood waiting for it to process his order, he leant against the wall, looking up to the ceiling. He overhears an officer talking to Captain Fisher, who was just about to leave to go home. "Any witnesses?" asked the officer.

"The perps husband, 2 friends and an officer. All are giving statements now. They've been brought here because the Northern Precinct currently have no holding rooms available. The husband and the 2 friends are quite understandably in shock. The husband had to be tranquilised. All are saying that the perp acted out of character".

James's ears picked up. *Out of character.*

James picked up his Styrofoam cup of coffee and walked over to the officer and Captain Fisher. He sips his coffee as he walks up to them. "Cap, mind if I get some details on this?" he asks Captain Fisher before acknowledging the officer.

"I already gave you a case earlier, James." Captain Fisher replied, frowning.

James nodded and lowered the cup away from his mouth "You did but it came back inconclusive."

James continued to explain that the statements and the footage were no help and the weapon had no prints other than Tim's. "However," James added, "one witness did say that Tim came back *acting out of character.*" James says the last 4 words slowly and deliberately. He looks between both Captain Fisher and the officer. Captain Fisher frowned and the penny dropped.

"You think they could be connected?" Captain Fisher asked.

"Could be," James says taking another sip of his coffee.

"Okay James, have a look at this, but I think Northern Precinct may have already sent a detective over there. Go over and talk to the guy and see what you can find. If it turns out that it has nothing to do with your case, then we'll give it back to whoever is heading it now. I don't want you doing too much too soon," Captain Fisher picked up his keys from the desk and headed towards the

SFPD doors, he turned to James, "and keep me informed as well" he said.

Detective Cross walked into the interrogation room. "Tell me what happened" James said as he sat down at the table.

"I've already been through this a dozen times!" Ryan said through gritted teeth, his eyes raw from crying.

"I know, I'm sorry but it *may* be connected to another case I'm on. That's all I can say for now. I understand you're upset. Please take your time and let's go through this one more time."

Ryan tells him all the details, starting from the plan of the night, how his friends were 20 minutes late, to deciding to get some candy for the movie from the store next to the theatre.

"What happened then? James asked.

"We went inside the store to get the candy, Eleanor stayed outside for a smoke. We were joking about which candy to get, then Eleanor walked in and grabbed hold of the guy and killed him. I don't know why. She's *never* had a violent bone in her body! Never! I… I don't know why she would do something like this! I can't understand where she got the blade from! Now she's… now she's dead." Ryan started crying again. James moved forward on the table.

"I know this is hard for you. Believe me I do." James said, sympathetically. Ryan looked up at him. Though his bloodshot eyes he told James that he has lost the one thing that ever gave his life any meaning.

A flash of guilt, anger and sadness hit James.

Kelly.

James shook away his emotions. "You are welcome to

leave when you like. I suggest you at least wait here till your friends are finished. It's not good for you to be alone right now." he managed to say as he patted Ryan on the wrist. He stands up and walked towards the door, opening it. He motioned for an officer to wait in the room whilst Ryan calmed down.

Arriving at the scene, he pushed past the onlookers and walked into the grocery store. Much like the bank, the whole area had been taped off. Although the bodies inside had been removed, the blood stains were still on the counter. There were a dozen cops and forensic officers. He noticed the manager of the store, a short sweaty squat man, who was clearly distraught talking to an officer. James walked up and introduced himself.

"I can't believe it." the manager said, shaking his head. "I just can't believe it. That poor boy, Matty! I only took him on 3 weeks ago! Thank God that officer was here and killed that bitch! My God, Matty... Why did she do it?! Why?!" The manager sounded understandably upset and frustrated.

"We are doing everything we can to determine that." James said. The manager frowned at James. "Why are you here anyway? There is already a Detective here. He's looking at the security footage in the back room." he asked

Detective James walked to the back room and gives a courtesy knock. A moment later the door opened and an unfamiliar face stares at James.

"Yes?"

James flashed his badge. "Detective James Cross of the SFPD Central District," he said.

The unfamiliar tall thin man with a gaunt face and a

blonde ponytail and a goatee, clearly disgruntled, flashed his badge back. "Detective Andrew Gates of the SFPD Northern District. Mind if I ask what you are doing here?"

James nodded. The last thing he intends to do is piss off Detective Gates if they must cooperate on this.

"Captain Fisher sent me down here as we suspect it could be related to the bank incident that took place earlier today," Detective Cross explained, still standing at the doorway. "If it turns out they are not related then of course we will not interfere and leave you to continue your investigation."

Detective Gates grunted, then nodded grudgingly. "Alright, alright. You better come in then." He said, stepping aside. In the small back dusty room that doubled as a stock room and security office, there were several large stacks of various stock piled up on one side and a single monitor and a recording device with 2 seats on the other side. Detectives Gates walked over and sat down, gesturing to the other seat for James to sit.

"I was just reviewing the outside footage from earlier. We have our perp walk up with her friends, and then they went inside. She stayed outside smoking and..."

James looks at him. "and what?"

Detective Gates leant forward and rewinds the footage and hit play. "See for yourself," he said whilst looking at the screen.

Eleanor and her friends were clearly seen outside the store. They were talking as they were walking to the entrance. The conversation inaudible. 3 of them went inside whilst Eleanor stayed outside smoking, standing next to entrance of the store. Nothing happened for 45 seconds apart from Eleanor constantly raising the cig to her mouth, taking a drag then blowing out the smoke. A hooded figure approaches

Eleanor from behind. Someone, who clearly didn't want to be seen. She has a moment of surprise on her face and turns around. As she spins round the figure raises their hand in front of their face and opens out the palm of their hand.

As if they were about to blow her a kiss.

"What the hell," said James quietly, as he moved closer to the screen.

"Just keep watching." Detective Gates said.

The hooded figure lowered their hand, and Eleanor and the hooded figure stand opposite each other, unmoving. Within a matter of seconds, the expression on Eleanor's face goes from shock, to confusion, to expressionless. After 30 seconds the hooded figure reaches into his pocket and hands Eleanor the serrated blade, which she slowly takes from his latex gloved hand and places in her handbag. She then turns around slowly. There is an officer approaching on the other side, who from the looks of it didn't notice what just happened. The dark figure backs away off screen. Both Eleanor and the officer enter the store.

Detective Gates looks at Detective Cross expectantly.

"Go back a few frames. Go back to when she turns around again." Detective Cross demands.

Detective Gates clicked on the backwards frames and hit play. The footage replayed.

Eleanor had a moment of surprise on her face and turned. As she spun round the figure raised their hand in front of their face and opened out the palm of their hand.

"Pause. Now zoom into the hand," James said, staring at the screen intently.

Detective Gates clicks the zoom button, getting closer one frame-by-frame. The gloved hand filled up the screen, although it is more pixilated now, it is still quite visible.

"What the hell?" Detective Cross whispered to himself. In the palm of the hand was a small mountain of white powder.

CHAPTER 5

The downtown neighbourhood known as 'The Tenderloin' had gained a dangerous and crime ridden reputation for drugs and prostitution. There are several theories as to how it gained its name, ranging from stories of a corrupt cop, who bragged that he could afford Tenderloin cuts of meat from all the extra cash he made on the side, to the more realistic theory that the 50 block neighbourhood had gained its name for being the "soft underbelly" of the city, due to the amount of corruption and illegal activity.

Tourists to the city are strongly advised to avoid the area, especially at night.

Lee Shaw, known only as Shaw to his associates, walked through the streets fully aware of its dangerous reputation, but also knowing that he himself had contributed to its problems, being a dealer on the streets for the past 8 years.

Last week, as Shaw was walking the dark alleyways, looking for potential addicts in desperate need of a fix, was approached by a man. The man had a shaved head, a short brown beard and didn't look like an addict in need of a fix. He appeared to be in his early forties and had piercing blue eyes. He had explained to Shaw that he has no interest in drugs, at least *his* drugs, but that he had a business opportunity. Believing it was a set-up, Shaw pulled out a blade. The man quickly grabbed hold of Shaw's wrist with his left hand and twisted it. Shaw dropped the blade in pain and the man grabbed him by the shoulder with his other hand, head butted him in the nose then punched him in the stomach, lifting Shaw off his feet and sending him flying against the brick wall behind him, sucking the air out of his lungs.

Looking around, the man bent down to Shaw and picked up the knife. Shaw was on the floor in a fetal position gasping for air, winded, too afraid to move. The man, still bent down over Shaw, tapped the blade deliberately, gently on Shaw's face tutting with each tap.

"Now… What am I going to do with you…?" The man said ominously. His icy blue eyes penetrating Shaw's soul as he stared down at him.

"Do I do the city a favour and rid this city of one more scumbag dealer, or…" he paused for effect, "spare you and give you the opportunity I was going to offer you before you tried to stab me?" He asked rhetorically. "Hmmmm" he continued to tap the blade on Shaw's face again, each tap becoming more forceful, the tip getting closer to his eye socket. With his left hand the man grabbed a handful of Shaw's greasy black hair and quickly pulled him up to a sitting position and slammed his head against the wall behind him. The sudden pain causing Shaw to momentarily lose vision, the man pushed the blade under Shaw's left eye and twisted it, threatening to pop the whole eye out of its socket.

"Pull a stunt like that again and I'll carve you up so bad even your own mom wouldn't be able to recognise your corpse… Are we clear?"

All Shaw could do was nod and mouth the word *yes*.

The man stood up and offered a hand for Shaw, who

was still on the floor against the wall "Come on. I'm not going to hurt you. Anymore." The man finished with a smirk. Shaw reluctantly took his hand and was pulled up onto his feet. The man didn't divulge what the business opportunity was but told Shaw an address and time. He said he had a few more people to speak to first. He also warned that if he told anyone else about this meeting he will know, and he will follow up on his earlier promise.

Walking to the meeting point, Shaw had an awful sense of trepidation. He had always thought that he could handle himself in any situation and that he wasn't scared by anyone, but there was *something* about this guy that scared the hell out of him. *Could be the fact he nearly beat your ass to death, Stupid!* He thought to himself. Bizarrely, and contradictorily, there was also something intriguing about the guy. Yes, he scared the shit out of Shaw, but he also had an air of self-confidence. Something that Shaw rarely saw in people. Curiosity had got the better of Shaw and he decided he will go to the meeting point. If he didn't like what this guy had to say, then he would just leave.

Even though it was nearly 2am the streets were full of people. Except they weren't the type likely to help anyone in need. More likely to assist the mugger than the victim. *Then* mug the mugger.

The building Shaw was walking to was in a run-down dilapidated area of "The Tenderloin". The buildings had long since been abandoned after the business's closed and most buildings were covered with graffiti.

As he approached the wire fencing that surrounded the graffiti covered, old decaying building, Shaw looked around to make sure no one could see him. He lifted the bottom corner of the grey mesh wire fence that had come away from the post and ducked underneath. Shaw got out his cell phone and turned the light on as he walked cautiously towards a set of dark blue double doors that had dirty cracked windows. He took a deep breath, slowly opened them and walked through.

Shaw continued walking down the darkened corridor towards the room at the end, using the light from his cell phone to help see in the darkness.

Shaw could hear slight movement from the room as he got closer to the door, but no talking. He peered inside. The room was lit by a battery-powered LED floodlight that sat in a corner of the room on top of a disused high cabinet. There were 5 other people either sat or standing alongside the walls. He switched the light off on his phone and walked in. They all stared at him in silence as he entered. Shaw walked to wherever there was a space on the wall and waited, eyes on the floor, not looking at anyone else. He waited till he felt everyone had lost interest in the newcomer then he quickly looked up at them, studying and regarding each person in the room and he could see that there were 3 males and 2 females. They were just like him. Drug dealers just like him. Most were wearing hoodies pulled up over their heads, just like him. Here because they were told to, just like him.

Wonder if they got their asses handed to them as well, just like I did? he wondered.

He scrutinized a bit closer. Then he saw the one next to him glaring at him as he was studying them.

"Wanna take a picture?" he said, scowling.

Shaw swiftly looked back at the floor and said nothing.

The same male, wearing a blank black baseball cap with a black hoodie pulled up over it, glared at Shaw for a moment longer before looking at the rest of the group.

"Screw this... I been here for 40 minutes already, the dude is a no show. I'm out." he said irritably as he went to make his way to the door.

"Patience is a virtue," a recognisable voice filled the room, coming from the doorway. Black cap froze, and slowly backed up to the spot he was standing in before, reassuming his position leaning against the wall. A tall figure of a man now stood in the doorway. The bright light coming from the floodlight next to the door blinding and prevented anyone from fully seeing the man, only a dark silhouette. As the man stepped inside, Shaw recognised him the man from the street.

The man walked to the middle of the room, looking around at the 6 drug dealers around him. He is wearing a black jacket, white shirt and blue jeans. He was also wearing blue latex gloves.

"Ladies and gentlemen," the man said loudly, looking at everyone. "thank you all for coming here. And, thank you for your discretion. I trust you all remember my promise to you if you would have told anyone about this meeting."

Shaw and the other dealers all looked at each other.

"I realize you may have been waiting a while," he said, shooting a stern look at black cap with disdain. "but I had to wait until you were all here to join the party. I had to stagger your arrivals as to avoid suspicion...

First, I believe introductions are in order. My name is Marcus. I have asked you all here because I have a little business proposition for you. However, I do not know your names yet and it would be foolish of me to enter any sort of business deal without getting to know my associates first."

Marcus Bovin pointed to a female, who appeared to be in her mid-20's and had a mostly shaved head, apart from two locks of hair either sides of her forehead. She wore a hoodie and she was stood nearest the doorway. "We'll start off with you. What's your name?"

"Sky." She replied.

"Sky...I assume that is a nickname?" he asked.

Sky nodded in acknowledgement. Short for her real name, Skyler.

"Nicknames are fine." Marcus confirmed, before looking at the male next to her, who also looked to be in his mid-20's and had a blue hoodie pulled over his head.

Marcus looked at him expectantly and held out his hands "Well?"

"Jackson" he said, chewing gum and rolling his eyes.

Marcus nodded then turned his head to next wall, at black cap.

Black cap kicked himself from the wall. "This is such bullshit. This ain't a church club where we're all friends and shit! I don't know any of you, and I don't want to!" he said, squaring up to Marcus.

Marcus didn't say or do anything other than stare silently at the dealer. Then with exaggerated panache, not unlike that of a maître d at an expensive restaurant, swung his hand out towards the door. "Then feel free to leave, I won't stop you." he said, before lowering his voice. "However, I assure you, you will regret it."

Unsure of whether that was a genuine statement or a threat, black cap, who looked about 20, stood still for a moment, before he made his way back to his spot against the wall once more.

"Hawk" he said, looking at the floor.

Marcus nodded, pissed off at him for being so insolent. Up next it was Shaw's turn.

"Lee Shaw… People call me Shaw"

"How's the nose?" Marcus asked with a smirk.

Shaw gingerly touched his nose and remained silent. Marcus then looked at the girl next to Shaw. She appeared no older than 17, a short girl with long dark hair, tucked behind a dark navy hooded jacket.

She stared back like a deer caught in the headlights.

"Come on, we won't bite," said Marcus.

"Alex," she quietly replied.

Marcus moved onto the next person on the other side of the wall behind him.

A coloured man in his late 20's, wearing a black hooded jacket, stared back. "Oakley," he finally said. Marcus nodded and then turned to the rest of the group.

"Right, now the formalities are out of the way, I'll shed some light onto why I invited you here this morning, in the simplest way possible," Marcus said, whilst looking at everyone in the room. "A while ago, I managed to obtain a drug, and I have managed to improve on it. I realise that you are all supposedly experts in this field, and wish for you to help me. I want you to use it and I want the whole damn city shitting itself over my drug."

"What kind of drug is it?" Sky asked.

Marcus turned around and smiled. "One unlike you will have ever seen before. I assure you."

"What would we get out of helping you?" Oakley asks.

Marcus turned around and faced him. "Not only will I compensate you all generously with the drug, but I guarantee it will help all of you in the long run. No more running from the police. No more looking over your shoulder. The police will be too busy shitting themselves about what will happen next to care about a few dealers here and there."

"Shitting themselves? Why would the police shit themselves over a drug?" Asked Shaw, frowning. Marcus turned to Shaw. "My drug *isn't* your typical drug. You don't take it yourself. At least I hope you won't.... You choose someone. You blow it on their face or spike their drinks. Then, your selected victim, become yours. Your slave. Your puppet. You will have *complete* control of them. It's perfect."

All the dealers looked at one another, unsure of what to say.

"What is it called?" Alex asked.

"It has many names where it comes from, but its street name is *Devils Breath*."

"Fucking bullshit."

Marcus scowled, turned and saw Hawk staring at him rebelliously.

"Ain't no drug like that I ever heard of. You expect me to believe if I give some asshole your shit that I will have complete control over them? How does it work? Where did you get it from? You can't answer cuz it's bullshit. YOU are bullshit. Fuck this, bitch." Hawk speedily crossed the room, purposely bumping into Marcus' shoulder as he did so.

Marcus sighed, shaking his head. "You are seriously starting to piss me off." He reached into his pocket and grabbed a small plastic bag filled with white powder, ripping it open. Marcus lunged for Hawks shoulder, spun him around and blew it directly into Hawk's face. Marcus quickly stepped back as to not inhale any of it himself. Hawk looked momentarily confused, then just stood still. The rest of the room watching in confusion as the events unfolded in front of their eyes.

As if to prove his point, Marcus opened his jacket, reached in and took out a gun. He looked at his audience one by one.

"Your victim" he declared. "will do *exactly* what you tell him.... Or her." He added. "you will have complete control over everything." Marcus held out the gun in front of Hawk. "Take the gun from me, Hawk."

Alex gasped as Hawk reached forward and took the gun from Marcus.

"Now, when I count down from five, I want you to shoot yourself in the head."

The whole room gasped when Hawk raised the gun and stuck the barrel under his chin. Marcus started counting, slowly.

"Five..."

"Four..."

"Three..."

"Two..."

Alex shouted "No!" as the same time a psychotic grin spread over Oakley's face. The others in the room are too shocked to do anything other than watch.

When Marcus loudly said "One." Hawk pulled the trigger.

Alex and Sky covered their mouths in shock. The look on Oakley's face turned from psychotic grin to disappointment as the gun in Hawk's hand clicked empty every time Hawk pulled the trigger.

Marcus laughed loudly as he snatched the gun from Hawk. "It's empty!" he said, amused. "I always expected that I'd have to prove my drug to you, so thought I might as well have a few theatrics with me to help me prove that point! Of course, I don't want to kill the people I want to help me... However, this one *has* been pissing me off tonight."

Marcus reached into his inner pocket on the other side of his jacket and pulled out a large knife "Hawk, take this knife, press the blade on the side of your face and pull it down."

Alex screamed in shock as Hawk obediently picked up the knife and silently ran the blade down the left side of his face, starting from the side of his forehead, down over his cheek to his under his chin, blood trickling down his face and onto his body as he yanked the knife down.

CHAPTER 6

Billy Lake picked up his Security badge, lanyard and keys and headed for his front door. He stopped in the hallway, looking at himself in the full-length mirror on the wall.

"How did you get so old?" He sighed to himself. He stared at the 73-year-old man in the mirror, who has short grey hair that colour coordinates perfectly with his uniform, which consists of a grey shirt with the red and black sports arena security emblem on the right breast, black tie, grey trousers and black shoes.

"What did you say?" his wife asks from the next room. "I didn't hear you!"

"Oh, nothing dear, just wondering where the damn time has gone and how did I get so damn old!" Billy grunted as he bent down to get his shoes on. His wife, Andrea Lake, walked from the kitchen into the hallway.

"Your time has gone into building a lovely home and family," Andrea said, "and your age has just matured you like a fine wine." she added as she stood in front of Billy and straightened his tie and kissed his lips. He looked lovingly at his wife, whom he had grown old with, together since they were childhood sweethearts. Whereas he had grown old through the years, the grey hair and abundance of wrinkles were the evidence of that, his wife had seemed to defy the aging process and still looked as good as she did when they first met.

Or maybe that's just what I see. Billy thought to himself.

Billy held both her hands together in his and looked down at them. Andrea sensed something wasn't right. "What's the matter?" she asked, concerned.

"I'm not sure." Billy sighed "It's probably just the jitters about next month. I don't know if I should just carry on or-"

"Billy, stop. We have been through this over and over again. You have been working there for 32 years and you should look forward to your retirement. I know you're nervous about it, but we will be fine. You should've retired years ago. We have enough cash saved up to set us up comfortably and enough in our retirement funds. I want us to spend some time together, before..." Andrea's voice trailed off.

Billy looked up at his wife and saw a hint of sadness in her eyes. *She's right. Of course, she is. She's a woman after all, if there is one thing I have learnt over the years is to never argue with a woman and that women are right... even if they're wrong* Billy thought to himself.

"I'm sorry dear, I just worry that I'm making the wrong decision, but you are right. I have been there for quite some time now. I guess I'm just institutionalised to the system." he said with a smile. Billy leant forward and kissed her on the lips. He then put his arms around her and hugged her gently.

The 52,564 seated sports arena that Billy worked at was just on the outskirts of San Francisco. It was home for the San Francisco basketball team and hockey team, though sometimes it was used to host music artists concerts. Its purpose tonight however was for the Monday night battle between the San Francisco Scorpions basketball team and their opposing team. Even though there were 2 hours before the game started, the car park was already half full by the time Billy parked up in the employee's area of the car park.

Billy strolled up to the security gate office and picked up his badge that was attached to his lanyard and flashed it at the guard behind the glass door. The guard smiled and leant forward to press the button that would allow Billy access to the office.

"Y'know you don't need to keep showing your badge to us every time you get to work Billy! I think we all know your old face well enough by now to know who you are! But why break the habit of a lifetime, eh?!" the guard chuckled as Billy walked in and closed the door.

Billy turned to the young guard who was sat down at the desk "Manners cost nothing Stephen, you'll do well to remember that when I leave." Billy said as he took off his jacket and hung it up in the corner next to the glass door.

Billy and Stephen looked at each other for a moment, before they both smiled and laughed. "You know I'm gonna miss you, old man. You taught me everything I know about security." Stephen said as Billy walked over and sat down next to him at the desk.

"Yeah I suppose I'm going to miss your ugly ass too." Replied Billy as he leant backwards in his chair, his arms stretched out upwards before coming together and resting on the back of his head, making Stephen laugh once more.

"Looks like it's going to be a busy one tonight, the car park is already half full of semi-tanked fans." Said Billy, looking at one of the many screens on the wall next to them.

Stephen nodded. "Yeah it's a full house. Not one seat left." He said, now also looking at the screens. "You know you're gonna miss this after you retire."

Billy turned from the screens and looked at Stephen. "I will, to be honest with you. I've been here a long time, son. I have seen things that most people would give their right leg to see. Hell, I've been working here longer than you've been alive!"

Stephen noticed a distant look on Billy's face, one that he had never seen before.

"Don't get all sentimental on me, ya lucky bastard. Just remember to drop by now and then." said Stephen to try and lighten the mood, and Billy's spirits. Billy smiled and chuckled. "Yeah maybe I will. If I get that bored that only your ugly ass face will brighten my day! Anyway, come on, we better get to our post to let the mad rush start to come in!" he said as he stood up from his chair and patted Stephen on the back.

At their assigned security gate check-ins, Billy is doing the body checks with a hand-held metal detector and next to him at a desk is Stephen is doing the bag checks. Both are looking for any alcohol and, of course, any weapons.

"We almost done here?" asked a tired Stephen to Billy almost two hours later.

"Yeah, I think so, only a few last late comers from the looks of it and that should be about it... why?" replied Billy, metal detector in hand.

"Because I'm busting for the bathroom! Been needing it since we got here!" Said Stephen through gritted teeth, looking flushed.

Billy let out a hearty laugh "My God Stephen your worse than me, and I'm an old man! Tell you what, we've just got these last few to process then you can go and *relieve* yourself! Okay?" Billy said.

Stephen nodded anxiously. Billy smiled, purposely taking his time scanning the last few people as to make Stephen wait a few more painful minutes.

"You can be such an ass sometimes Billy!" said Stephen loudly as he ran off to the restroom.

Laughing to himself, Billy waited. Even though it was against protocol to only leave one guard at the check-in during "processing", as soon as the main crowd were inside, it was unofficially acceptable. Checking his watch, Billy didn't notice the coloured man walking up to the security check in till he was standing right in front of him.

"Oh, I'm sorry, sir! I was in a world of my own!" said Billy, standing up. By the time he had picked up his metal detector and walked round to the man, he didn't see Oakley grab a handful of *Devils Breath* from his pocket.

"You don't seem very dressed for your team, if you don't mind my saying." Said Billy as he noticed the man was wearing dark jeans and a dark hooded jacket that was pulled up over his head. Billy bent over and started to scan Oakley, starting from his legs. Billy slowly worked his way up, eventually reaching Oakley's waist. Billy straightened up now and he ran the metal detector over Billy's front and then round the back.

The metal detector beeped and vibrated intermittently.

Billy frowned. "Sir, do you have anything you'd like to take out of your back pocket?" he asked.

Oakley turned and raised his latex gloved fist quickly to Billy's face, opened his palm and blew *Devils Breath* directly into it. Billy stumbled backwards a few steps, then stared back, unmoving.

Still unsure of whether *Devils Breath* would actually do what Marcus said it would, such as *have complete control*, Oakley smiled, "bark like a dog" he demanded. He almost keeled over with hysterical laughter as Billy started to bark with a deep voice.

"Oh shit, oh shit, oh shit, this stuff is awesome!" Oakley said, chuckling. "Okay you can stop barking now". Billy obediently stopped barking immediately. Still chuckling to himself, Oakley picked up the bag and opened it. Then he gave Billy his instructions.

As the buzzer signalled the start of the game between San Francisco Scorpions and the Chicago Cheetahs, Billy walked around the perimeter of the side-lines. He then turned and slowly walked right into the middle of the court, interrupting the game. A wave of boo's came from the spectators. All the players from both sides immediately stopped playing and looked at each other confused. One of the Chicago Cheetahs players marched up to Billy.

"Hey man what's your problem?" he asked.

Billy turned and looked the player straight in the eye, reached into his pocket for the gun that Oakley had given him, pointed it and shot the player in the face. The screams and shouts filled the entire stadium as both players and fans alike tried to run or hide for cover. Billy pointed the gun and randomly shot into the crowd of fans and at the players around him, not caring who or what he hit. The more shots that were fired, the louder the screams become.

"BILLY! STOP!" Shouted Stephen, who was running and barging past the frenzied crowd. Billy spun round and faced Stephen. Billy quickly reached into his other pocket and gripped the knife that Oakley had also given him. Before Stephen could react, Billy had run at him and plunged the knife deep into his belly. Stephen grabbed hold of Billy's hand, shocked and scared at what was happening. Billy then raised his gun hand and shot Billy in the throat, killing him instantly.

Stephen's body fell to the floor. More Security guards fought their way through the crowd towards Billy. Surrounding him, they ran at Billy all at once and eventually managed to subdue him and take the weapons from him before he could harm anyone else.

CHAPTER 7

Detective Cross was sat on his couch in his apartment, sipping a large mug of coffee in his right hand. The pictures from the bank and shop cases spread out on the table in front of him. In his left hand, he was holding a printed picture of the zoomed in open hand with the mound of white powder. To avoid distraction, James had turned the picture of himself, Kelly and the bump around, facing it the other way.

He usually worked from the precinct for this kind of work, but he just needed... Hell, truth be told, he didn't know what he needed. One minute he needed to be at the precinct with other people around him, next he just needed to be alone.

Right now, it was the latter. Back at the precinct, one of the officers had walked over to his desk and offered his condolences. James's eyes instantly filled, he gulped and said thank you, then excused himself to the bathroom to compose himself. As nice and friendly as it was, the unexpected gesture was like a punch to the gut. That's when he knew had would be better off at home to continue his work.

One by one, Detective Cross studied all the pictures, trying to make some sense of it all. Two random people, approached by someone (*Who*?!) and had something blown into their faces (*What?!*), then they behaved as though someone was pulling their strings (*How?!*).

James raised the mug of coffee and gulped a mouthful as the cell phone next to him sprang to life, ringing loudly, causing James to jump, spilling the coffee down his shirt.

"Shit!" he cursed, wiping the stain as he placed the mug on the table. He irritably picked up the ringing phone and looked at the caller ID. Captain Fisher.

"Hello Captain Fisher," James said, trying to sound not pissed off. "I'm just looking at these pictures, trying to work-".

"I know James," Captain Fisher interrupted. "There may be another case that has come up that may be related to them."

"What?" James sat up. "Where?"

"The basketball stadium just outside San Francisco," Captain Fisher replied. "Security guard shot up the stadium as soon the game started. Killed 5 people, injured many more. He was eventually overpowered by the other security guards and passed out soon after. He's been taken to St. Mary's hospital."

James frowned, and shook his head "That's terrible Captain, but I don't see how it's related to my case."

"The security footage shows the security guard searching someone, then they blow something into his face. They also gave him a knife and a gun. *Whoever* this guy is, was wearing a hoodie that was pulled up so it covered his face and he kept his head down the whole time, so we can't get a full facial recognition."

James picked up the image that he had printed of the hand holding the white substance. *What the hell is it?*

"I think you should head over to St. Mary's now to be

there when he comes to."

"On my way now, Sir." Said James as he stood up and hung up on Captain Fisher. He bent down and, whilst looking at the scattered photos, picked up the mug, but knocked the picture of him, Kelly and bump off the table. James's heart jumped into his throat, and there was a pang of sadness as he heard it smashing as it hit the floor.

He knelt to pick it up and, turning it over and saw that there was a large diagonal crack over the picture. He held it close and ran his fingers over Kelly. His heart ached whenever he thought of her. And the baby he never got to hold. His eyes filled and he wanted to cry again. He had never felt such loneliness like this before. It felt like all the pain and anger he was feeling was destroying him internally. He let out a whimper as a single tear escaped and ran down his face. But he knew deep down he had to be strong. He couldn't let this destroy him. He had to get better. For himself. And for Kelly.

He placed the damaged picture down, went to his bedroom to change his stained shirt, and went to the hospital.

CHAPTER 8

"How many have we done now?"
"Not enough idiot! No way near our quota!"
"Well then hurry, Hector! He will be here soon!"

The Mexican chemists argued in their own language, hurriedly chopping, grinding, weighing and measuring the drugs in front of them, the same way they had been trained to.

They were in a large room that was partitioned off into 4 sections. This is where they had to work, sleep, eat and shower for the last two months; the only access to fresh air was from a small window on the other side of the room, the area where they had to sleep in sleeping bags on old used mattresses. The largest section was the area they are in now, the area that which they work. The other smaller "rooms" were partitioned in a row at the back, which as well as a bedroom, consisted of a bathroom and a kitchen.

Marcus had travelled to Mexico looking for out-of-work chemists. He eventually had found three willing job seekers, giving them an up-front payment of $1000 each and promising them $10,000 at the end, as well as being promised food and lodging during their stay. The only catch being that they cannot tell anyone where they were staying, what they were doing, and they are to remain contained in the same building until the job is done. Together, along with Marcus, they had perfected the effects of his drug.

But this had become their prison.

Classical music blared out from a small radio behind them. Hector and Jorge were sat at a large metal table that was full of trays lined neatly in a row, measuring scales and cutting utensils. Both were wearing white face masks, blue rubber gloves and white overalls that covered their entire bodies. It all looked very clinical.

"Shit! I think I can hear him coming! We should wake Roberto!" Hector whispered in Spanish, wide eyed.

Before Jorge had chance to run to the other side of the partitioned room to warn Roberto, the main door that led to the world outside was unlocked and swung open. Marcus Bovin stepped inside. He reached into his side pocket and pulled out a white face mask and pulled it over his head and face. Both Hector and Jorge stood frozen to the spot as Marcus approached them around the table.

"Good evening gentlemen. I trust you have met today's quota, especially after yesterday's disappointment." Marcus said.

Hector gulped and remained silent, looking down at the ground. Jorge finally spoke up, mumbling out of fear.

"Apologies sir, but we haven't met it again today. Roberto was too sick from exhaustion, so he is sleeping. Hector and I have tried our hardest to fulfil the quota. We will not rest until we have." Jorge mumbled in his own language.

"Roberto is sleeping?" Marcus asked, in a sinister tone.

Hector and Jorge knew better than to answer him. They just nodded.

Marcus scowled. He understood Spanish, but seldom

spoke it. Without saying a word, he walked through to the kitchen area of the room. A short moment had passed before he reappeared holding a kettle that had steam emanating from the spout.

"Silencio," Marcus mouthed, walking towards the sleeping section.

Quietly walking into the bedroom section and stepping through, Marcus looked at Roberto in the corner on old dusty mattress. Marcus walked quietly, calmly over and stood next to Roberto's sleeping body. He raised held the kettle full of boiling water above him, then he slowly tipped it, pouring the contents.

The boiling water seeped through his few layers of clothing instantly.

Roberto's eyes snapped wide open and he saw Marcus standing over him pouring the bubbling contents of the kettle over his crotch. Roberto bellowed so loud it hurt his lungs, but that was nothing compared to the boiling water that was scalding his skin. He desperately tried to move out of the boiling cascading waterfall, but Marcus kicked him back down and positioned the kettle, so it now poured over Roberto's naked stomach, instantly scorching him. Roberto's scream increased even louder. Roberto continued his frantic attempts to move out of the way, but Marcus stopped pouring and stamped on his stomach again. Marcus started pouring again, moving the kettle further upwards Roberto's body, leaving a trail of blotched, blistered skin in its wake. By the time the kettle now was positioned over Roberto's head and face, the kettle was now empty.

Roberto lay on the soaked mattress, screaming and shouting incoherently.

Hector, Jorge and Roberto were sat at the small table in the "kitchen" area of the room. Roberto was pale and whimpering, clutching cold wet rags over his body to try and soothe the pain of his damaged, blotched skin. In front of them stood Marcus Bovin, his furious face red with rage.

"I will not give you any more chances." Marcus said in a low, but sinister tone. "I have been more than fair with you all. I bought you all in to do one job for me. This is your last fucking chance... Hector, your mother. She is in hospital, yes?"

Hector's eyes widened. *"Yes sir, how do you know this?"* he asked worriedly in spanish.

Marcus didn't answer, but looked at Jorge

"Your wife, she works at a garment factory in *Méjico*, yes? Jorge's horrified expression confirmed it.

Marcus smiled nastily at the mortified faces of the Mexican chemists in front of him.

Both Hector and Jorge were now suddenly pleading with Marcus.

"How do you know this?!"

"No! Please don"t hurt our families!"

"¡SILENCIO!" Marcus shouted above the pleads.

Both men went quiet, fearing for their families safety.

Marcus looked finally at Roberto, who had his head down and eyes closed mumbling quietly to himself whilst holding the now dry rags to his skin.

"And Roberto... Don't you have a 12-year-old daughter?"

Roberto looked up, terrified.

"I have to say that's a *very* busy road outside her school. It'd be a shame if she was involved in an accident whilst she was walking to school. Don't you think?" Marcus sneered.

"*No please! Don't do anything to my Maria!*" Roberto starting pleading.

"Gentlemen, this I promise you. If you do not improve, you will *never* see your loved ones again. Did you really think when I asked you to work for me that will not have some sort of insurance?"

In broken English, Hector begged. "Please... please... do not harm our families. I am sorry we have displeased you. If maybe we can just get outside, we-"

"You are *not* leaving this room until I deem it so." Marcus interrupted. "You all knew what you were signing up for before you came here. You will all be rewarded when this is over. You will have an overwhelming amount of money to take home," Marcus said, in a intimidating tone. "*but* if you do not start producing what I am paying you for, your family will be the ones to suffer. That, I promise you."

CHAPTER 9

After Detective James Cross received the phone call from Captain Fisher, he had gone to the hospital, but Billy Lake hadn't woken up. James stayed as long as he could, but after 3 hours of walking circles in the corridor and endless amounts of coffee, he had decided to call it a night. James had told the on-duty officers who were keeping watch to call him as soon as Billy wakes up.

It was about 5pm the following afternoon when James's cell phone rang.

Detective Cross politely knocked on the hospital door and opened it. As he poked his head through first, he saw an old man lying in bed.

"Hello Billy, I'm Detective Cross," he said, showing Billy his badge as we walked in and closed the door.

Billy sat up in bed, with one hand locked in handcuffs to the bars on the side of the hospital bed.

"Finally! What the hell is going on here?! I wake up, chained to a damn hospital bed and no one telling me what's going on! Not the nurses, doctors or that useless officer outside! Where is my wife?! Why the *hell* am I here?!" Billy demanded irritably, waving his free arm around in frustration.

"You don't remember?" James asked as he pulled up a chair next to the bed.

"Remember *what*?! Tell me why I'm here!"

"What's the last thing you *do* remember?" James asked patiently.

Billy frowned. "What? Why?" he asked, exasperatedly.

"Please Billy. Just tell me the last thing you remember. I'll give you the answers soon."

Billy gave James a frustrated look. "Fine but you better tell me what the hell is going on!" he sighed. "I had spent the day with Andrea, we had a walk around the park and a lunch together, then we went home so I could get ready for work at the stadium. It was one of my last shifts before..." Billy paused.

"Retiring?" James added.

"Yes..." Billy frowned and nodded slowly "Yes I had work with Stephen, and we - we..."

James leant forwards on his chair "Try, Mr Lake."

"We were working together at the gates and then he left to go to the bathroom. Someone came up to me to be processed but..." Billy clenched his eyes shut. He slammed his free hand up against his forehead in frustration. "I... I can't remember what happened!" he said through gritted teeth.

"You sure you can't remember anything else?" James asked.

Billy clenched his free hand into a ball and held it to his forehead. "I was searching him, and the metal detector started beeping. Then... then..." Billy growled in annoyance. "I'm sorry I don't know anymore!"

"Can you tell me what this man looked like?"

"I- I can't. I can't remember. I'm sorry. Why? Did he do something?" Billy asked, alarmed.

James coughed, clearing his throat and leant closer to

Billy. "He didn't Mr Lake. You did."

Billy frowned as James spoke.

"I'm afraid we have reason to believe you were drugged with something, an unknown substance, and coerced you into doing something terrible, Mr Lake."

The colour quickly drained from Billy's face. "Oh my God! What happened? I... I don't remember any of it! Is Andrea alright? Did anyone get hurt?" he asked, worriedly.

Detective Cross stared into Billy's unblinking eyes. "Yes Billy. I'm afraid people did get hurt." He sighed. "The suspect gave you a gun and a knife. After he gave you the weapons, he left the stadium. Leaving you to walk into the middle of the stadium, and..." Detective Cross hesitated briefly. "open fire."

Billy's eyes filled with tears as James spoke.

"Five people were killed and many more were injured, either by you... or by trying to escape. Mr Lake, I'm sorry to say, but one of the victims killed was Stephen." James let that last sentence hang in the air, studying Billy's reaction. Billy stared into space, not saying anything for nearly a full minute, then he slowly turned to meet James' eyes.

"I'm sorry," Billy mouthed as the tear-filled eyes began pouring down his aged face.

It was 10pm by the time Detective Cross left the hospital. Billy was that distraught over the incident he had to eventually be sedated by the hospital staff. The news of what he had done had taken its toll and he kept shouting for his wife. James had stayed for a further hour, hoping to talk more to Billy, but that was to no avail as he passed out 15 minutes after being sedated.

James called Captain Fisher on the way out of the hospital, relaying everything that had taken place.

"And he can't remember a damn thing?" Captain Fisher asked frustratedly down the phone, before sighing. "Damn... anyway, good work James. Now get some sleep and I'll see you in the morning at the precinct. I'm pulling an all-nighter."

On the way home James walked past an open bar. Slowly he turned around and looked at the doors. Deliberating whether to walk in or not, he looked at the time on his watch.

22:18... *too late* he thought as he shook his head and turned to head towards home, before he stopped again.

Screw it. One drink won't hurt. Not after everything I've heard today. He thought as he turned back to the entrance.

Slouched over the bar, James raised his hand. "Another double whiskey" James said tipsily, hailing the male bartender over.

"Sure thing" the bartender said, grabbing the glass from the bar and replacing it with a fresh one. Then he grabbed the twenty dollars that James had left next to the glass.

"Keep the change." James slurred. He had been drinking alone for best part of an hour, not saying a word, other than to order more drinks.

"Thanks man!" the bartender grinned as he poured the whiskey, without measuring it, and placed it in front of James.

James sat looking at the glass for a full 10 minutes before he picked it up and placed it to his lips. In one mouthful he drained the entire glass. Slowly he turned around on his stool to survey the bar. He was one of the few people inside. There were 2 other people in a booth opposite busily talking and another person wearing a hooded jacket with the hood pulled up over a black cap sat at a table on his own near the restrooms. James considered walking over to talk to him, seeing as they were both alone. He stood up but instantly felt the effects of the whiskey and had to sit back down again.

Hell with it… I'm not that desperate he thought as he turned back to the bar to order another drink. The barman was busy serving another customer. James dropped his head and waited.

"James?" a familiar voice spoke.

His head shot up and looked around, but he couldn't see anyone other than the barman and the three other patrons. He shrugged and dropped his head again, closing his eyes.

"James?" the voice spoke again.

That voice again. "Kelly?!" James replied, desperately.

"James, you can't keep punishing yourself like this,"

"But I wasn't there for you!"

"You were there, all the time James. Whenever I needed you,"

"I wasn't there when you *really* needed me though, when Sean Conner drove into you. I wasn't there when he got in that car drunk and killed you and our baby! I wasn't there…"

James began sobbing quietly.

"James, you have to forgive Sean, otherwise you won't ever be able to move on. Please James. Get better. For me."

"Sir?"

"Kelly! I'm so sorry!" James was still sobbing heavily. "I- I should've been there for you! I'm sorry baby! I'm so sorry!"

"Sir... are you alright?"

James opened his tear-filled eyes and looked up. He saw the bartender with a concerned look on his face. James wiped his tears away and nodded.

"Do you need me to call you a cab to take you home?"

"No. No thank you... I'm ok. I think I might have had one too many." James said shaking his head and faking a smile "I'm gonna take a leak, and head home."

"Okay. Take care man." the barman said picking up James's empty glass and wiping the bar where the glass sat.

James drunkenly turned on his stool and headed for the bathroom. He saw that the guy who was sat on his own was no longer there but standing by the bathroom door looking restless. James walked by and noticed that underneath the black cap and hoodie he had what looked to be a fresh scar running down the left side of his face. *Scarface* James amusedly thought to himself. After James had taken a leak, he washed his hands then walked out of the bathroom. He noticed that someone else had entered the bar now and was talking to Scarface. He eyed them suspiciously as they seemed to be talking *too* quietly and quickly. James sat down at a table and pretended to look at a bar menu as he watched the two of them. Sensing that some sort of drug deal was about to happen, he readied himself. The new man reached into his pocket and pulled out a handful of cash and was about to hand it to Scarface.

Wait till I see the drugs James thought to himself as his police training kicked in. As the new man held the cash out not-so-discreetly in front of him, Scarface reached into his back pocket and pulled out a bag of white powder.

Detective Cross shot up from his chair, knocking it back onto the floor.

"POLICE! FREEZE!" James shouted, holding out his badge and reaching for his concealed gun. The two men both looked momentarily surprised before Scarface cursed and kicked a table over towards James. The new man picked up an empty glass and threw it at James's head, missing him and smashing against the bathroom door. James ducked out of the way and when he looked back up both men had run towards the bar doors. He was about to run after them when he noticed that, in all the commotion, they had dropped the cash and the bag of white powder. He quickly grabbed the bag and ran out of the doors, into the cool night sky.

Looking left and right to see which direction they had taken; he couldn't see anything down either sides, other than an empty street lit by streetlights. Then he heard shouting on his right, in the distance. He reached for his gun and ran quietly, staying as close to the buildings as possible, hiding in the shadows. As he got closer, he could hear the shouting.

"You stupid ass punk ass bitch! You dropped it! What the fuck?!" Scarface yelled.

"Not my problem, man! I get caught with that shit on me, then that *would* be my problem. Gettit?! Ain't no way I was gonna get caught with that shit!" the other voice retorted.

Detective Cross arrived at the building next to the side street where the shouting was coming from. He backed up close to the building as possible to avoid detection and thought about calling for back up, but by the time it arrived, they would be too late so he decided against it.

He took a deep breath and spun around the corner, his gun raised.

"Freeze! Do not move!"

Both hawk and the other guy raised their arms. "Shit", Scarface muttered, his arms in the air.

James kept alternating his aim and reached for his handcuffs. The man who had walked into the bar waited for James to switch his aim and bolted down the side street next to them.

"Freeze! I said freeze!" James shouted, taking the gun off Scarface. This momentary distraction prompted Scarface to run in the opposite direction, further down the side street they were in.

"Shit!" James said through gritted teeth, changing direction, running after Scarface now. Knowing he was too drunk to keep up, he shouted "Freeze!" one last time.

James raised his pistol, aimed and fired.

CHAPTER 10

Knowing better than to fire his weapon at someone when intoxicated, Detective Cross fired it into the air, hoping that would be enough to encourage the running suspect to freeze. Unfortunately, it wasn't, Hawk had escaped.

Running down as many dark side streets as possible, Hawk eventually slowed down and stopped, crouching and hiding behind a large metal dumpster. He leant against the wall breathing heavily catching his breath. Now he had lost the cop, Hawk pulled the phone out of his pocket and dialled the number. Holding the phone to his ear, Hawk gulped nervously as it rang.

Hawk had woken up in a small puddle of blood, his face in such pain. He was still in the same room, but he couldn't remember what had happened. He touched the side of his face and grimaced. He pulled his hand away and saw blood on his fingers. He groaned loudly as he struggled to his feet. Walking over to the door and, as he grabbed the handle, it was pushed open from the other side. Marcus walked in and Hawk backed off, fearfully. He couldn't remember exactly what had happened, but he definitely sensed that Marcus had something to do with it. Marcus explained that, because of Hawks attitude the previous night, he had used Devils Breath on him to prove to the others what it can actually do. They others were in awe at Devils Breath after witnessing it themselves and soon were willing to take some off Marcus. Marcus also explained that, if Hawk changed his attitude, he too can have some.

"Yes?" the voice answered.

"Marcus, its Hawk. I need to see you man, something's happened."

"What's happened Hawk?"

"I… I lost the Devils Breath. I need some more."

There was silence on the phone for a few seconds. "No problem. Meet me at the same place as before, in the same room. I'll give you some more Devils Breath."

"Okay man, on my way there now."

The phone hung up and Hawk walked over towards 'The Tenderloin' side of town to meet Marcus.

Hawk walked into the same building as before, towards the same room he had met Marcus. Again, the only source of light was from the room at the end of the corridor. Hawk walked inside expecting to see Marcus, but there wasn't anyone there. Hawk walked to the wall and leant against it, waiting.

After twenty minutes, Marcus walked in, closed the door behind him and looked straight at Hawk.

"Tell me what happened." Said Marcus, quietly. Hawk looked away from Marcus and at the floor, unsure of how to tell Marcus he tried to sell the Devils Breath.

"Well I…" Hawk began saying nervously "I thought that if I could sell it on to some other dealers I know, that maybe it might spread a bit faster. Y'know, like, you wanted the whole city to be shittin' itself, so the more dealers who have this drug can cause more shit an stuff!" Hawk said, pleased with himself for trying to put a spin on it.

Marcus nodded. "I see. So, you were trying to do me a

favour?" he said.

Hawk smiled. "Yeah! Yeah, I was trying to do you a favour!"

Marcus didn't smile or didn't show any emotion whatsoever. "Okay, so how come you told me you lost it?" he inquired, walking back to the door and locking it. Hawk was looking at the floor again and didn't notice.

Hawk began hyperventilating, his heart thumping.

"Well y'know..." Hawk hesitated, "there was a drunk cop that tried to jump us when the deal was going down. I thought that being in a quiet bar near midnight in a quiet part of town that it'd be okay, y'know, the bar was empty! We were about to make the exchange when the cop jumped us, and we managed to escape, that- that's when we lost the Devils Breath. I'm sorry man! The cop caught up with us again outside, but we got away again. He was too drunk to keep up with us". Hawk was hoping that was a good enough explanation and he could leave as soon as possible. Marcus stood about a foot away from Hawk, silent, breathing heavily. Hawk suddenly felt more intimidated than ever. "So then, can I have some more Devils Breath?"

Marcus nodded slowly, reached into his pocket with his left hand and pulled out a bag of Devils Breath. He dangled it in front of Hawk.

"My product," Marcus said, "is completely unique. The way I have crafted it to perfection means that it works instantly on its victim. As you well know." Marcus gestured at the scar down the side of Hawk's face. Hawk looked down at the floor

"Listen man, I gotta go." His voice quivering as he spoke. "Can I just get that and go?"

Marcus smiled and said, "Of course, Hawk."

When Hawk reached for the bag Marcus swung his right arm up and struck Hawk's jaw. The sudden blow knocked Hawk off his feet and onto the floor. Marcus kicked Hawk in the stomach. He then bent down and threw the open bag of Devils breath over Hawk's face.

"You have disappointed me Hawk. On your feet." Marcus growled. Hawk slowly stood up and vacantly stared into space. Marcus turned to the cabinet in the corner of the room, opened it and pulled out a gun.

CHAPTER 11

Detective Cross walked into the Central District precinct and went straight to Captain Fisher's office. He stood there for a moment, trying to compose himself so as not to appear too inebriated then, after taking a deep breath, he raised his fist and knocked on Captain Fisher's office door.

A voice boomed from the other side. "Come in"

James opened it and walked in. A tired looking Captain Fisher was sat at his desk, in front of him on the desk were several empty Styrofoam cups of coffee amongst all the paperwork.

"James! What are you doing here?" Captain Fisher said, surprised. James slumped down on one of the chairs opposite the desk, looking ashamed. "I-err- got a confession to make Cap." Captain Fisher leant forward on his desk and held his hands together. "Okay, what's happened?" He frowned as the smell hit him. "Jesus! You stink! Have you been drinking again?!"

James cleared his throat and replied "Yeah…"

Captain Fisher sat back in his chair to avoid the alcoholic fumes. "Smells like you've been bathing in the stuff! So, what's this confession you have? Or is that it; That you've had a drink? If it is, you really don't need to-"

"No Cap, that ain't it." James interrupted. "I was in the bar, I was about to leave and I saw a drug deal going down.

I tried to apprehend the dealers, but they got away,"

"You tried to make and arrest whilst drunk? Jesus James!" Captain Fisher piped up.

James continued. "Well they ran out of the bar and I was about to chase after them when I saw they had dropped this," James said, pulling the bag of white powder out of his pocket and throwing it onto the desk. Captain Fisher took it and eyed it suspiciously. "I'll have it analysed. Anything else?" he asked.

James cleared his throat again. "After picking up the bag I chased after them and eventually caught up with them, I tried again to arrest them, but they got away again. I... I even fired my gun, into the air, hoping that would be enough to get one of them to stop."

Captain Fisher's face dropped. "Goddammit James! You fired your weapon whilst drunk?! What the hell were you thinking?! *Anything* could've happened!" he said furiously.

"I thought that maybe it might be something to do with my case." James sighed.

"And what if it isn't?! Huh?" Captain Fisher gestured to the bag of white powder on his desk "What if you just risked your life and someone else's just for a tiny bag of cocaine? Jesus James!" He frowned and shook his head. "You fired your gun whilst drunk!" he repeated. "What the hell are you doing drinking anyway? I thought you were trying to quit?" Captain Fisher asked, standing up.

Detective James looked up at Captain Fisher across his desk, his eyes filled with tears, and dropped his head. "It's just so hard Cap, I miss her so much." he quietly mumbled.

Captain Fisher's furious expression softened, and he walked round the desk and sat down on the chair next to

James.

"She should be here Captain. Kelly and my baby. They were both taken away from me." James mumbled. He put his face in his hands and started quietly sobbing. Captain Fisher placed his hand on James' shoulder and went to speak.

A soft knock on the door interrupted them, and the door opened. An officer walked into to ask something when Captain Fisher looked up from the chair and raised his free hand to stop him. The officer looked momentarily surprised and he realised he walked in at an uncomfortable moment. The officer mouthed the word *Sorry* and then he backed out, closing the door. Captain Fisher looked back down at James. His hand still resting on James shoulder.

"Shit," captain Fisher sighed. "I'm sorry James. I thought you could handle being back at work. I thought it'd be good for you. I am so sorry, son."

James raised his head and wiped his face with his sleeve. "Captain… I'm fine. Seriously. Please don't take this case away from me Sir. Don't… Please…" he mumbled.

"James, look at yourself. You're falling apart. I think it may be best if you get some help." Captain Fisher said, genuinely concerned.

James cleared his throat, trying to stop the tears from forming "Cap. I am fine. I fucked up. I'm sorry. Do not take this case away from me." he pleaded.

Captain Fisher exhaled, removed his hand and stood up. "James, I truly don't know what to do with you. Maybe you do need to be here. Maybe you don't. We'll talk in the morning." he walked round to his desk and picked up his keys. "You're staying in one of the cells tonight."

"Am I under arrest Captain?"

"Don't be a smart-ass James. You're in enough trouble as it is. You're staying in the cell till you've sobered up." Captain Fisher stopped and shook his head. "Goddammit, James. Do you think you could give a detailed description of the suspects, before you pass out and forget?"

"Yes Cap. Well one of them at least. He had a scar running down the left side of his face."

"Good. Now go find Officer Hoyt and tell him all the details so he can let the other precincts know, just in case. Now get out of here." Captain Fisher replied, clearly frustrated.

CHAPTER 12

In the early hours of the morning, Hawk limped through the streets, bloodied, bruised and beaten, carrying a black backpack. The few people that were up and about gasped at the grim sight of him and walked around him. One kind-hearted woman did notice and, unlike other people passing by, marched up to him to see if he was okay.

"Oh my! You Poor thing! What happened?" She asked, reaching for her phone in her handbag. "Do you need an ambulance? You look like– Hey!"

Hawk barged straight past her as though he hadn't even seen her, almost knocking her to the floor.

"You asshole!" she called out when he didn't stop or turn around to apologise.

Hawk carried on and stepped into the busy morning traffic and walked across, not looking or paying any attention to the cars that had to slam on their brakes, swerve to avoid him and crash loudly into each other. Drivers angrily got out of their vehicles, shouting at each other, motioning at their cars and gesturing at Hawk. Hawk continued, as if nothing had happened, staring straight ahead, walking to the building he was told to go to.

Walking up the steps towards the building's main

doors, Hawk screamed within himself as he desperately fought to stop. Tears filled his eyes as he reached the doors and pushed them open with his right hand, his left remaining in his pocket.

Inside the busy San Francisco Police Department lobby, no one noticed Hawk at first as he limped through the doors. He stood still for a moment, not saying anything as officers and detectives either sat at their desks, on the phones, typing away frantically at the computers, or walked briskly by with armfuls of paperwork.

Hawk stepped forward and a skinny young blonde female officer looked up from her desk. The look of the grotesquely beaten man that had just walked into the precinct caused her to jump up from her seat.

"Sir? Are you alright?" she asked as she speedily walked up to him. Hawk didn't answer and continued past her. "Sir, do you require medical attention?" she asked again as he limped by. The young officer frowned and followed Hawk. "Sir! Do you need any assistance?" She repeated more firmly and loudly.

The shouting caused the noise to quickly die down as every head turned towards Hawk as he walked deeper into the lobby. He was now in the middle of the room, surrounded by cops and detectives, who now all and stood and watched as Hawk walked amongst them, all sensing something wasn't right.

"What the hell happened to you?" A deep voice came from a detective standing at the right of Hawk. "Sir, you will be forcibly detained for your own safety if you do not respond."

Hawk trembled and attempted to speak, but instead pulled his left hand out of his pocket.

Less than a second later every officer and detective

had their guns pointed at him, shouting orders at him all at once.

"DROP THE WEAPON!"

"DO NOT RAISE YOUR FUCKING HAND!"

"YOUR MOVE DICKHEAD-"

"YOU DO NOT WANT TO DO THIS!"

Many more were shouting at him, although he could not hear as they were all yelling together.

Hawk stood still, holding the pistol given to him by Marcus. He looked straight ahead and then took a long slow breath.

Then he raised his hand.

Every officer and detective had shot at least once, puncturing Hawks body in multiple places, before he fell to the floor dead.

CHAPTER 13

"Rise and shine, sleeping beauty!"

James lay on the thin mattress and cotton sheets. He slowly opened his eyes, groaning as the light felt as though it was piercing his brain. He covered his eyes with his hands, sighing.

"It's your own fault son," Captain Fisher chuckled, placing a Styrofoam cup of hot black coffee down on the floor next to the bed "Get your ass up and get washed. You can use the bathroom at the back. Then come and see me. I have some news for you." He said as he walked out of the cell, closing the door behind him.

Twenty minutes later Captain Fisher was sitting at his desk, shaking his head as he reread the paperwork in front of him.

"Un-fucking-believable" he muttered to himself.

There was a knock at the door, and then it slowly opened. James walked in, looking slightly fresher, although not feeling it, holding the now semi-warm cup of coffee.

"Sir, I am so so sorry about last night." James said uneasily, walking towards the desk.

Captain Fisher kept his head down and raised his eyes from the paperwork to look at James. "Sit down," he said. His eyes shifted back down to the paperwork.

"Yes sir" James replied, worried that the Captain had just ignored his apology. "Have you been here all night?" James asked, trying to change the subject.

"Nope. I was gonna be, but then you turned up blind drunk. I went home after you gave a description of the suspects. I thought it best if I come in first thing instead." Captain Fisher replied, still looking at the report in his hands, "Anyway, pay attention. We have the results back from what you obtained last night. It seems that you actually managed to find something quite vital to your case."

Detective Cross blinked, unsure of what to say. "Okay," he settled with. The feeling of relief instantly swept over James. The outcome could have been much worse if it had just been a common bag of cocaine. "What is it?"

Captain Fisher leant forward and placed the paperwork in front of James. "Scopolamine."

"It's *what*? James frowned, picking up the paperwork, glancing at it but not actually reading it.

"Well, it is actually a complex mixture of drugs, but it is largely a drug called *Scopolamine.* Ninety-seven percentile to be precise. The rest is one percent cocaine, one percent methamphetamine and, believe it or not, one percent pain killer, all of which, according to the report, act as an accelerant to the scopolamine."

James sat back in his chair, confused. He placed the paperwork back on Captain Fisher's desk. The hangover still hovering over him. "What the hell is Scopolamine? I've never heard of it?"

Captain Fisher huffed and shook his head, "That doesn't surprise me. I hadn't either. I had to look it up myself. It has several names for it. Scopolamine. Burandanga. Hyoscine. But the most common name for it is *Devils Breath.* It's really horrible stuff. Jesus H. Christ!" Captain Fisher slammed his fist on the table, "James, the DEA want to get involved. If we don't get this sorted soon then they will move in and take over. I really don't want them guys down here."

James squeezed the bridge of his nose and closed his eyes tightly, struggling to comprehend the impact of what Captain Fisher was saying.

Captain Fisher sighed, "Basically James, Devils Breath hypnotises people. It completely removes their free will, leaving them vulnerable to whatever the assailant wants them to do, essentially turning their victim into a mind-less slave, whether it is to rob them, rape them or worse.

It leaves their victim somewhat coherent and articu-late but with absolutely no control over what they say or do. And they have no memory of it afterwards either. What is more, it is completely tasteless and odourless.'

Detective Cross shook his head, dumbfounded. "Where the hell does it come from though?"

Captain Fisher picked up his report. "It is mostly ob-tained from the Borrachero tree, that is common in Co-lombia, where reports of criminal activity involving this Scopolamine is more common, and it actually goes way back, the more I look into it. The latest thing I found about it is that; it is said in ancient times the drug was given, forcefully I imagine, to the mistresses of dead Co-lombian leaders and were told to enter the mass grave of their masters.... Where they were buried alive."

James' eyes widened. "Holy shit" he said whispered.

"My thoughts exactly, James." Captain Fisher con-tinued reading extracts from the report, "apparently, during the cold war the CIA experimented with it as a truth serum but was quickly abandoned as it caused powerful hallucinations. As deadly as it is, it is actually used in a number of medicinal practices, albeit in very small dosages." Captain Fisher placed the reports down on his desk.

"Scopolamine," Captain Fisher sighed again. "is also in a plant called Jimson Weed, which is grown in most of Northern America."

James understood immediately but didn't say anything.

"It seems that we have someone who has learned to harvest it, and has crafted it into something deadlier as, like I said earlier, the complexity of the other drugs speeds up the effects and works instantly."

Detective James was just about to open his mouth to speak when someone knocked on Captain Fisher's door. A middle-aged female cop opened and walked into the office. "I'm sorry for interrupting Captain Fisher, but I think you should know that someone matching Detective James' description of the suspect he chased last night just walked into the Eastern District Precinct."

Both Captain Fisher and Detective James exchanged startled looks and turned back to the female officer.

"Do they have him in custody?" Captain Fisher asked. Both he and detective Cross stood up in unison.

The officer shifted on her feet. "No Sir. When he walked in, he pulled out a gun. They had to shoot him."

"Goddammit!" Captain Fisher looked from the officer to Detective Cross. "We should go over there and take a look." Detective Cross nodded. Captain Fisher looked back at the officer. "Anything else?"

"One more thing Captain, he was also carrying a backpack full of narcotics. Looks like bags of cocaine."

CHAPTER 14

The car slowed and came to a stop outside the steps of the busy school. Many people of mixed ages, teachers and students alike, were walking across the road up the steps and into the school, or were either stood outside in groups, talking and laughing. Some of the older kids were smoking, despite being told repeatedly that smoking on school premises is prohibited and anyone caught doing so shall be punished. The teachers knew that the students would find a way to smoke at some point of the day, so most chose to let it slide.

"Have a great day sweetie! Pick you up after school! Love you!" Katie Swann said loudly to her 12-year-old son, Josh, as he was opening the car door to get out.

"MOM! Not so loud!" He snapped back quietly, glancing around him to see if anyone had heard.

Katie chuckled at his embarrassment. "I suppose you're too cool to give your momma a kiss before school now?"

"Mom!"

Chuckling again at his awkwardness. "Fine, what about an 'I love you' back?" Katie said.

Rolling his eyes, Josh quickly scanned around himself again, making sure the coast was clear. "*Okay*! I love you too mom!" he muttered quickly and quietly.

Satisfied that she had successfully embarrassed her

son, Katie switched the engine on. Josh was just about to slam the door shut.

"Josh!" Katie shouted.

"Now what, mom?!" Josh said, clearly getting irritated.

"You forgot your sports kit." Katie said, reaching into the back seat and handing it to him.

Driving back from the school, Katie was about to take the right turn which would take her home, when she had remembered there were some groceries she had to pick up.

"Darn it!" she said to herself as she indicated left instead to take her to the grocery store.

Pulling into the car park, Katie reached into the back seat for her handbag after parking up. She reached inside and got out her grocery list, got out of the car and made her way into the store.

Walking down the cereal aisle with her trolley, Katie was working her way down the list and looking at all the boxes of breakfast items. "Why does Josh have to be damn fussy?!" she said to herself as she picked up a box of his favourite cereal, which happened to be twice as expensive as the other boxes, she chucked it into her trolley, which was now half full. Katie walked out of that aisle and turned the trolley to her right, checking her list as she did so and bumped her trolley into a young girl, who was wearing a hoodie pulled up over her head.

"Ouch!"

Katie quickly looked up, startled. "Oh! I am so sorry! Are you alright?!" she said, walking up to the girl.

"I'm okay, just banged my knee! I'll be alright. Don't

worry." The young girl said, smiling.

"Okay," Katie replied, feeling slightly silly and care-less. "sorry about that. Are you sure you're alright?" she asked, walking back round to her trolley.

The young girl just smiled and nodded.

Down the next aisle, Katie was checking out the loaves of bread. She was about to place it in her trolley when she looked back and noticed the young girl down the same aisle, who quickly looked away as soon as Katie noticed her. Deciding not to ask for a third time if she was okay, as she didn't want to make a big fuss, Katie pushed her trolley down and round to the next aisle. She picked up a jar of coffee and turned to place it gently inside as she didn't want it to smash. Katie saw again the young girl, who again turned away when Katie noticed her. Starting to feel unnerved, Katie pushed her belongings past the girl, who kept her head down as Katie was passing by. As Katie was walking by, she kept her eyes on the young girl, then she looked away towards the end of the aisle.

"Excuse me?"

Katie turned to speak but instead turned into a cloud of white powder. Then she went to talk but lost all ability to do so. Then she lost the ability to move her body.

Alex looked around, frantically, to see if anyone saw what happened. To her relief the store was quite empty. Alex looked at Katie, who just stood still, silently.

"How far do you live from here?" asked Alex.

"Fifteen minutes away." Katie involuntary replied, al-most robot-like. Tears formed in her eyes as she tried to internally fight.

"Is there anyone else at your house?"

Katie shook her head.

"Will there be anyone coming back to your house soon?"

Katie shook her head again.

"I want you to drive me to your house, give me all your jewellery, valuables and whatever money you have lying around, then drive me into town. Okay?"

Leaving the half-full trolley where it was in the store, they exited the store together. Katie walked to her car, with Alex trailing behind, constantly looking around to see if anyone noticed. Nobody did. They approached Katie's car and Katie slowly fished the keys out of her pocket and pressed the button to unlock it.

Alex wondered whether it would work, getting someone to drive whilst under the effects of *Devils Breath*. To Alex's surprise, Katie drove just as normal as anyone would have driven sober. The drive itself was quiet. Alex kept glancing at Katie, scrutinizing her blank and vacant expression whilst she drove. Alex began to wonder how it must feel; to have the freedom of movement and speech completely taken away from you, to become someone's puppet on a string. No sooner had these thoughts entered her head, they were just as quickly dismissed when the car pulled into a quiet suburban neighbourhood. A long row of houses on the left side of the road and a large park on the right. Katie drove down to the end of the row of houses and gently pulled to a stop. To Alex's relief there was nobody around. Katie obediently sat still, staring straight ahead, now and then Alex noticed her right eye would slightly twitch.

I wonder if she is trying to fight it, Alex thought.

"That your home?" Alex asked, pointing to an impressively large house.

Katie's right eye began twitching more as she nodded her answer.

Alex felt a pang of jealousy as she gawked at the house, which deepened the more she looked at it. She had never, ever seen a house this big and would never live in one like it either.

Suddenly this became a whole lot easier for her.

"Right then," Alex said, turning to Katie "We are going to go into your house, and you will load this car with as much valuable stuff as possible. I'm talkin' jewellery, money, cameras, laptops... then you will take me into the city so I can sell that shit. Ok?"

Katie didn't answer, but silently got out of the car and walked up to the front door, holding the front door key. Alex got out the car and, not bothering to close the car door, followed closely behind Katie, just wanting to get this over and done with quickly.

Alex's jaw fell open as she walked in.

HOLY SHIT! JACKPOT! she thought as she followed Katie through the front door. The front door led straight into the impressively large foyer of the house and the stairs, which were to the left of the door, spiralled up round the length of the foyer to the upper right side.

Surely a place like this needs a cleaner! Alex thought to herself. To the right of where Alex was standing was a large table, which an assortment of shoes and trainers were messily scattered underneath, and on top was a small granite bowl, presumably for keys as there was just a single key in the centre of it for the time being. Next to the bowl was an expensive looking silver letter opener. Alex whistled joyfully to herself and turned to the table. She picked up the bowl and tipped the key out. Alex held the small but heavy bowl up to her face and studied it briefly to determine whether it will make any money.

Screw it! She thought as she stuffed it into her jacket pocket, which only just fit. Alex picked up the letter opener and stuffed that into her other jacket pocket as well.

Katie reappeared and walked down the stairs carrying a large bag of jewellery. She walked straight past Alex and out towards her car. Alex followed outside and watched as Katie placed the bag in the passenger side of the vehicle.

"Good Morning Katie! How's your day so far?"

Alex spun round and saw Alan, Katie's next-door neighbour, standing directly outside the house next door.

SHIT! Alex thought, fearfully as Alan now began to walk slowly over after Katie completely ignored him and walked back towards the house.

"Katie? Are you alright?" His friendly smile now turned into a frown. Katie walked straight past him and into the house. Alan turned to Alex.

"Is she okay?" He asked curiously.

"Yeah, she's fine!" Alex said, trying to sound as though everything was normal, "Katie just has a lot of stuff on her mind right now. Probably best if you come back later." She added, hopeful that he would just turn and leave. Katie walked by them carrying Josh's laptop, games console and her husband's digital camera to the car.

Alan shook his head. "No. Something doesn't feel right. Who are you?" he asked as he observed Alex suspiciously.

There was a momentary pause as Alex tried to think of an answer. "I'm Katie's niece. Aunt Katie is helping me out with something. We really are busy right now, so come back later!" Alex said forcefully.

Alan, looking at Katie as she walked past them both again and into the house, nodded. "Fair enough. Tell Katie to pop round once she has done here." he said, walking away.

Alex exhaled a sigh of relief.

"Just one thing though," Alan said, turning around and pulling out his phone from his pocket. "I have known Katie for years, and I know she is an only child." he said, unlocking his phone.

`I-I'm actually her husbands' niece!" Alex replied, panic returning.

"Oh, Mike! You should have said! That makes much more sense!" Alan said, smiling and laughing.

"Yes Mike!" Alex said, trying to remain as calm as possible. "Uncle Mike and Aunt Katie." She said, faking a smile.

The man dialled some numbers on his phone. "Thing is, sweetheart, Katie isn't married to anyone called Mike. Now, you have five seconds to tell me who the hell you are and what is going on here,"

Alex started to back off, panicking "No, no, no, no!" she began muttering.

"Now you stay right here!" Alan demanded as he hit *dial* on his phone.

Alex turned to run to the park when she felt Alan grab her by her left arm. Alex spun around and with her right arm, pulled out the letter opener from her pocket and swung it at Alan. The blade missed him by inches. "What the FUCK?!" Alan shouted, wide eyed.

"Let me go!" Alex screamed at him, still pulling away, trying to free her arm. Alex yanked her arm causing Alan to drop his phone.

"Who are you?! Tell me what is going on here!" Alan yelled at her.

A voice came from Alan's phone on the floor.

Alan looked down momentarily.

Alex swung her foot up and kicked Alan in his crotch. Alan doubled over in pain and, as he did so, Alex swung the letter opener upwards and stabbed him in in his right eye. There was a small popping sound as Alex yanked the blade back out. Alan fell to the floor clutching his face, screaming in agony, blood oozing quickly over his hands and body.

"Y-YOU FUCKING BITCH!" He screamed, blind and writhing in pain on the floor.

Alex stood over him and reached for the granite bowl in her other pocket, holding it above her and slamming it down on Alan's head. To her surprise, the bowl didn't break. Alex held it above her and slammed it down again, with even more intensity and ferocity then before. Alex repeated it one more time before Alan fell silent.

Katie, meanwhile, had carried on obediently filling her car with more valuables whilst all this was happening.

CHAPTER 15

Detective James and Captain Fisher got back in the car to drive back from the Eastern District Police Precinct after confirming that it was definitely the suspect that James had chased from the bar the previous night.

"Why the hell would he walk into a precinct full of police officers with a gun? It just doesn't add up! And *why* with a backpack-full of Scopolamine?" Captain Fisher asked frustratedly, turning they key, switching on the ignition.

"Beats me cap" James replied, reaching over his shoulder, pulling the safety belt across himself and buckling up. "You think he was looking for me?" He asked, half joking.

"Seriously James, this is bad. Why do you think he done it?"

James shrugged his shoulders. "Honestly, I don't know, sir.... It could be that he wanted to leave San Francisco with the drugs but changed his mind and really did want to find me for fucking up the deal last night? Maybe he's the one who started this whole thing, creating this souped up drug and I botched up the deal of a lifetime?"

Captain Fisher pulled out of the car park and started driving back to the Central Precinct.

"Maybe," Captain Fisher said through pursed lips. "I don't want any more of this shit in the streets! Can you imagine what it would be like if it did?! And if the DEA get involved then that's my job practically fucked. Goddammit!" he said, punching the steering wheel as he did so.

After a few minutes of silence, James turned to Captain Fisher. "One theory," James said thoughtfully. "is that *maybe* this guy himself was drugged? If this *Devils Breath* stuff can do what you told me, then maybe he was under the influence himself and was *told* to go to the precinct. Maybe there is still more out there,"

"God, I hope not." Captain Fisher said quietly as he gripped the steering wheel even harder.

Back at the precinct, Captain Fisher and Detective Cross were walking to Captain Fisher's office when an officer approached them.

"Officer Barnes, What's the problem?" Captain Fisher asked.

"Sir, you might want to hear about a report that came in a while ago. A man was attacked and killed outside his neighbour's house."

"Christ," Captain Fisher sighed, "well thanks but I already have a shitstorm to deal with. Why are you specifically bringing this to my attention?"

Officer Barnes cleared his throat, "Because it appears that his neighbour may have been drugged with whatever it is you're looking for. The house had a hidden security camera outside. When the victim was being attacked his neighbour, whose house it was, carried on filling up her car with her valuables without attempting to intervene."

Captain Fisher's eyes grew wide. "Well who alerted the police?! Surely someone must have seen something?! Send me the footage immediately!"

Officer Barnes nodded. "Yes sir. It has already been sent to you. The footage showed the attacker running from the premises. A cleaning service, which the home-owner must have previously arranged, turned up 20 minutes later. They are the ones who found the body and alerted the police. The lady was *still* outside her house, filling her vehicle with her valuables. When they tried to stop this woman, she became aggressive and passed out."

CHAPTER 16

Detective James Cross followed Captain Fisher into the office. Captain Fisher cursed as he slammed the door shut behind them. Although he knew that he should be more concerned that there is now a killer on the loose, Captain Fisher couldn't help but feel more anxious that *Devils Breath* was still on the streets.

"James! What the hell are we going to do?! It looks like your goddamn theory might be correct after all! Where the hell is this coming from?!"

James sat down on the chair next to the desk and shook his head. "I don't know." He said truthfully. "This whole thing is a fucking mess. We got shit happening all over the city because of this."

Together they watched the footage from the house. They saw Katie's car pull up outside the house in the distance and saw Katie get out of the car and walk towards the house. Following behind her was (what looked like) another female wearing a hooded jacket with her hood pulled up. She never looked up near the hidden camera so they couldn't fully ID her face.

After watching all of it, Captain Fisher stopped the footage and turned to James, speechless. James exhaled loudly. "Well that was intense!"

"You ain't kidding! Jesus!"

Detective James leant forwards and rewound the footage to the one and only time the hooded girl faced the camera.

James zoomed in frame by frame.

"So, where do we go from here?" Captain Fisher asked. "until this woman wakes up, we have no idea who this is," he said as he gestures to the girl onscreen. "and that's even if she remembers anything, which is doubtful! And now we have a goddamned killer on the loose!" he threw up his hands in despair.

Detective James didn't say anything but gazed in contemplation at the hooded girl onscreen. Captain Fisher broke his thoughts. "James! Did you hear what I said?" he said, exasperatedly.

"I'm thinking about something."

"Well, if it's going to help by all means share because I'm fresh out of ideas to where to even start on this one!"

James turned to Captain Fisher. "Think back to the grocery store case. The surveillance footage had shown a *hooded* someone blow this stuff into the victim's face. Then at the basketball stadium. Again, the footage from that shown a *hooded* figure blow it into the victim's face. Then in the bar last night. I chased down someone wearing a *hooded* jacket. That same person also dropped this stuff."

Captain Fisher nodded silently, looking at the hooded girl onscreen, and started to understand what James was saying.

Detective James took a deep breath. "I have an idea, but you might not like it."

James outlined his idea to him.

"I don't know James," Captain Fisher said, perched on

his desk, rubbing his chin. "you're asking to discriminate people by their clothing. The press will have a goddamn field day!"

"Then what do you propose?" James replied, more strongly than what he intended. "Pretty soon there will be another incident because of this stuff. You think we should just tell the press about it and hope for the best?" he asked rhetorically.

"Hell no! There would be all kinds of people claiming to be under the influence of this stuff if they got caught! But we *cannot* start arresting people just for their clothing."

"It would only be for a limited time. I'm not saying arrest them, but politely ask if they can empty their pockets and search them. If they don't have anything to hide, then they should cooperate. If we find anyone with any narcotics or contraband other then what we are looking for, depending on the class, we confiscate them and let them off with a caution. Then within, say, three or four hours we haven't found anything we formulate another plan. It's the only idea we've got right now."

"It's a terrible idea."

"But it's still an idea. Captain, there is a chance, a *small* chance, that this could work if we made it a sudden thing. If we just sit here talking about it, planning out all the details to the whole precinct for hours, then there is a chance it could leak and whoever has this drug may catch wind of it and change what they are wearing."

"Are you suggesting that we have crooked cops?"

"I'm only suggesting mistakes happen."

"Incompetent then,"

James quickly stood up. "You know what sir, forget it. You assigned me to the bank case, and this is where it is leading to. This is the *only* idea that we have right now. If you can think of another one soon let me know." He said as he turned to the door and grabbed hold of the door handle.

"James, stop." Captain Fisher said, looking tired. "I'm sorry. You're right, as unorthodox as it is, it is the only idea we have right now. *If* we go ahead with this, it will only be for two hours-"

James interrupted "Two hours?! With all due respect, that's not much of a time frame, sir!"

"Two hours or nothing." Captain Fisher sighed. "I'm going to have to make a public statement at the end of it as well. I won't say the exact reasons why we are doing this. Just tell them that we're doing it for the safety of the public and we appreciate the cooperation and patience of everyone involved."

Half an hour later, the whole precinct had been briefed and so had the other San Francisco precincts. To patrol the whole city looking for anyone they deemed conspicuous. Some of the police officers objected to this plan as they felt it was too judgemental of the SFPD to question citizens just because of their clothing but still, they followed their orders.

An hour and a half later a dozen or so people had been questioned all over the city. Most had been cooperative. Others had argued back saying they had the right to wear whatever they wanted to wear. Even citizens who hadn't been questioned or hadn't been deemed suspicious had argued with the officers saying it is highly unfair and in-appropriate to treat people like this.

Surprisingly, only three had minor narcotics on

them, which had been confiscated and one person was found with a small blade, which had been confiscated and the person was given a caution, much to the officer's grievance. He wanted to take him into the precinct.

"You better hope this works James," Captain Fisher said, peering out the window and seeing a handful of protesters outside. "people are starting to get pissed off with this plan."

"I know sir. They will understand if they knew."

"You better hope so. You plan only has a half hour left and, so far, we have no one in custody."

Down one of the many side streets in "The Tenderloin", Shaw had just sold some weed for the third time today. He lit one up for himself and took a long drag on it and held it in his lungs for as long as he could, savouring the taste and effects of the drug. He still hadn't used his bag of Devils Breath that Marcus had given him and, truth be told, he had no desire to either. He had no interest in harming or robbing anyone.

Finishing off the spliff, he stamped it out and picked up his rucksack, which contained several bags of cannabis and cocaine, and also one bag of Devils Breath. He walked out of the side street and made his way to the bus station to head home, a grotty and rather dirty apartment just outside of the city, but it was home, nonetheless.

He waited patiently at the bus stop, rucksack on the ground next to him, and he saw two police officers across the street, talking amongst themselves. He also saw them turning to look at him now and then. Sensing they were talking about him, he picked up his bag and turned to walk away.

Screw this shit, I'll get the next bus.

Turning around he noticed that the cops were no longer on the other side of the street but were now behind him following him. Speed walking, Shaw turned down an alley and started to run. The cops quickened their pace, both in pursuit. Shaw shrugged his bag off his shoulder and threw it in a dumpster he ran by, hoping to get rid of anything that could incriminate him. He quickly turned down another side street, hoping there was either a way out or at least somewhere to hide. There was neither. All there was, was a high brick wall with nowhere to go. A dead end. Shaw was trapped.

One of the cops turned down the corner and quickly closed their distance on him.

"You could've made this a whole lot easier on yourself if you hadn't ran!" panted the officer.

"I haven't done anything wrong! You have no fucking right to chase me!"

"We'll see about that. Empty your pockets and place both your hands on that wall." ordered the officer.

"Go ahead," Shaw said, emptying his pockets and throwing the contents, his wallet and his phone, on the ground and turning to face the wall. "You won't find shit because I don't have shit."

"Is that so?" said a new voice. Shaw turned and saw the other officer, who was also out of breath from running. He also had something in his hand. "Then why did you try to get rid of this?" he said holding up Shaw's rucksack.

CHAPTER 17

Overall 19 people had been questioned in the two hours, and only one had been detained. Captain Fisher had made a statement outside of the precinct to an audience of 16 people, which consisted of protestors and the press, claiming they had received calls from the public demanding answers as to why the SFPD were discriminating citizens purely based on their clothing and appearance. Captain Fisher had explained that their plan, although unorthodox, was necessary because it had worked. He also explained the current situation meant he was unable to divulge as to why they had to take such drastic steps.

Lee Shaw, who was usually confident, was sitting in the interrogation room, which consisted of nothing more than one table and three chairs, unsure what was going to happen to him. The chair Shaw was sitting in was purposely uncomfortable, making him move constantly, trying to ease the discomfort. Detective James and Captain Fisher were in the room next door, watching him through the two-way mirror.

"Told you it was worth a shot," James said, smiling with satisfaction and Captain Fisher.

"Yeah, yeah. Don't push it James." replied Captain Fisher, annoyed but was admittedly relieved it had worked. "So, how shall we go about this? This is your call."

James looked surprised. "Sir?"

"Your plan worked. Despite my doubts it paid off. It's only fair that you make the next move. Besides, it is *your* case."

"Thank you, Sir. That means a lot."

Captain Fisher didn't say anything. He just looked from James to Lee, and then from Lee back to James.

James chuckled. "I guess I start by talking to him," he said.

"I'm not saying a word till I get my attorney." Lee said.

Detective James Cross sat opposite Lee in the interrogation room, the only difference was that James' chair was much more comfortable. "You'll get your attorney. But we can talk in the meantime, can't we? Where did you get this substance – Devils Breath – From?" he asked.

"I told you, I want my attorney."

"And I told you, he is on his way. This would go much more smoothly for you, if you just cooperate. Did *you* make the drug?"

Shaw scoffed. "Like I could make that. I can barely make breakfast for myself."

James smiled. "So, who did make it then?"

Shaw looked at James and didn't reply.

"Right. Attorney." James said, nodding. "But we will get the information we need sooner or later. Why wait? Sooner you cooperate with us, the sooner we can deal with it."

"You mean the sooner I open my mouth the sooner you can lock me up."

James didn't say anything to that. He looked from Shaw and then glanced at the two-way mirror. He knew that Captain Fisher would be watching. He had an idea and decided to run with it. He looked back at Shaw.

"You should know that you aren't the only person we detained with this Devils Breath drug."

Shaw's mouth fell open. He looked shocked and went to speak. Captain Fisher quickly opened the door to the interrogation room.

"Detective Cross, may I have a word?" he asked sternly.

James stood up and walked out of the room. Captain fisher closed the door after him.

"What the *hell* are you doing?! We have no other suspects in custody, and we have no goddamn attorney on the way either!" Captain Fisher said through gritted teeth, clearly pissed off.

James held up his hands. "I know, but this kid doesn't know that! Look, I think we could get him to talk," he pointed to Shaw through the two-way mirror, "If an attorney got involved then this could take days. Time is a luxury that we don't have. I have an idea and I think it could work. Please Captain, trust me."

Captain Fisher looked through the mirror, then back at James, scowling. "Goddammit. This could be one expensive lawsuit if the kid decides to press charges when he realises there's no attorney on the way. I hope you know what you're doing."

James exhaled a sigh of relief. "I don't think this kid would have the brains to press charges," he said walking back to the interrogation room door.

"Like I said before. We have another in custody with

possession of the Devils Breath. I have talked to my superior and we are prepared to make a deal with the first one to give us the information we need." James lied. "Whoever speaks first will be considered as a cooperative and will have their sentence shortened significantly, maybe even placed in a low-security prison to serve their sentence. It ain't exactly a vacation but, believe me, compared to the others you could be sent to, it is a hell of a lot easier."

He stood up and walked to the door. He grabbed hold of the door handle and turned back to Shaw. "You both have twenty minutes before the offer expires and then you'll both be charged for possession of the rest of the narcotics you had, which by all accounts, was a hell of a lot."

Shaw sat alone in the room, trembling. *Who else have they got here?!* He began to hyperventilate. *If they talk first, then I'm fucked! I wouldn't last 5 seconds in prison! But if I do talk first, then I'll be considered a snitch!*

Captain Fisher and Detective James watched from the other room, Shaw was sweating profusely, they had turned the temperature up to maximum, to further Shaw's discomfort. This psychological tactic is used in order to get criminals to confess quicker.

After nearly twenty minutes, Shaw was now covered in sweat, his clothes were sticking to his body. He was breathing rapidly and looked extremely anxious.

James walked over to a water cooler on the opposite side of the room and poured a large plastic cupful of ice-cold water. He looked at his watch. "Showtime".

James walked back into the interrogation room, the

heat hitting him instantly. Straight away he wanted to turn and go back to the air-conditioned room he had just left. The thought of being stuck in this heat for the next few minutes, let alone for the past twenty, made him feel nauseous. There was also an intense smell of sweat. He sat down at the table and held the cup of water close to his mouth. Another psychological tactic.

"Have you thought about our deal, Lee?"

Shaw stared at the glass of cold water, the condensation on the outside of the cup looked heavenly. "Yes! Yes I have! I'll talk! I'll talk! Can I just get a glass of water?!" Shaw said desperately, the heat making him intensely faint.

James leant across the table and gave Shaw the cup, which he gulped down immediately. A look of instant satisfaction spread across his face. "Can- can I get another?"

"After you have told us what we want. Who gave you this stuff Lee?"

"I don't really know him. A couple of weeks ago, he came up to me and said he had a proposition for me. He wanted me to meet him at an abandoned building in 'The Tenderloin'. There were others there when I got there. Then he came in and told us about this stuff and that he wants us to use it to cause as much shit as possible, he never said why. I swear to you, I swear I wasn't going to use it on anyone. I had *no* interest in using it."

"Do you have a name?"

Shaw inhaled. "He said his name is…" he stopped and hesitated.

"Remember our deal, Lee."

"His name is Marcus."

CHAPTER 18

Marcus Bovin hung up the phone and walked into the room at a hurried pace, causing the chemists to jump as he did so.

"Relax Gentlemen, I am not here for you... providing you are on track for today's quota?" Marcus spoke in Spanish as he walked in. A look of relief spread over the chemists faces as they all glanced at each other and nodded.

"Si, Señor, Si." Jorge nodded.

"Good, good," said Marcus, speaking in English now. "I trust you all remember what happened last time you disappointed me?"

Roberto wrapped his arm around his scarred body and grimaced in pain. They all nodded, fear returning to their faces.

"I have some business to attend to soon. I believe that our time together may be coming to an end sooner than I expected."

The chemists looked at each other again, a look of confusion apparent on their faces. In broken English, Hector spoke. "But, *Señor*, does this mean that we will be returning to our families? With our payment?"

Marcus silently observed his chemists and, after a moment, nodded. "Sure. But let's not get ahead of ourselves. We still have work to be done first."

With newfound hope, all three chemists enthusiastically got to work.

Back in the same room, in the same abandoned building they had all met in before; Sky, Alex, Jackson and Oakley were waiting, tempers already flaring, talking loudly to each other.

"Man, I wish I never got involved with this! The goddamned police are everywhere looking for this shit! It was *never* this bad before!" Oakley said.

"I know! This guy said – he *said* that the police will be too busy looking for this shit to bother with us! It's worse now than it's ever fucking been!" Jackson reached into his pocket and pulled out one of the bags of Devils Breath and held it in the air, "I swear man, I swear I'm gonna shove this stuff right up-"

"Right up where?"

Jackson, spun around, quickly lowering his hand and hiding the Devils Breath behind his back, suddenly quiet.

Marcus Bovin stood in the room and shot a stern look at Jackson. He took a step forward. "I asked you, right up where?"

Jackson stared at the floor, refusing to look up. "I – I – only meant that -"

Taking his eyes off Jackson, Marcus observed the rest of the room. "You must understand, this situation was of course going to get worse before it got better," he said, going back to the doorway, picking up a large burlap sack and walking with it to the centre of the room.

"Of course, the police will always have made finding my drug their priority. But due to unforeseen circumstances, I admit it has happened quicker than I anticipated. The most observant of you may have noticed that we are now two dealers down."

Marcus bent over with the sack.

The rest of the dealers looked around at one another as the realisation hit them.

"Now, I'm not going to go into details," Marcus said, opening up the sack. "but Hawk and Shaw won't be joining us anymore. Rather than using my product like I asked it to be, Hawk tried to gain from it instead. I tried to fix the situation to buy us some more time, but it seems like they have San Francisco's "finest" on the case. As for Shaw, I have tried several times to contact him. I have a feeling he may not be as loyal to me as I hoped he would be."

Marcus tipped the sack upside down and emptied it.

The dealers looked at the pile of clothes on the floor.

"Right now, the police are looking for anyone that fits a certain description. They're pulling aside anyone just because of their clothing, questioning and searching them, looking for my drug. Unfortunately, I think this may be the case with Shaw. I called you all here as soon as I could. So," Marcus gestured to the dealer's clothes. "clean yourselves up, change your clothes and make yourselves less conspicuous. Then I will tell you where we go from here.

CHAPTER 19

Detective Cross scoured both paper-files and the SFPD network system files, searching for anyone with the first, or last name Marcus. In frustration, he slammed his fist on the desk, causing nearby officers to look over at him. He stood up and walked briskly to Captain Fisher's office, knocked, and entered before there was a reply.

"I couldn't find a thing on that name Lee gave us!" James threw up his hands. "Not one damn thing!"

"Think he gave you a false name?" Captain Fisher asked, sitting at his desk.

James shook his head. "No. No, he was – is way too scared to give me a bullshit name."

"And he didn't have another name for this Marcus?"

James shook his head again, irritated.

"What about any other names? Lee cannot be the only one this *Marcus* gave this drug to. There has to be other dealers who Lee can name?"

James looked at Captain Fisher, sighing. "Unfortunately, no. It seems that the *only* name he is willing to give up is Marcus. He won't give me any other names no matter how much pressure I put him under. Damn kid's got loyalty to his fellow dealers. I gotta give him that."

"Still, not much use to us if we can't find this Marcus supplier. What's your next move?"

"I'm working on it. I have an idea."

CHAPTER 20

"Sir, may we have a word with you please?" The Doctor asked.

Marcus sat next to the hospital bed, holding his sleeping fathers hand. He looked up at the doctor who walked in, who was then followed in the hospital suite by a nurse and another man, who was wearing a dark suit.

"Err, Yeah. Sure. What's this about?" asked Marcus, making no effort to stand up.

"Sir, we would rather talk in private if we may. This is rather a sensitive nature." The man in the suit replied.

"And who are you?" Marcus asked, irritation starting to creep into his voice. "I know the doctor and the nurse, but I have no idea who you are?"

The man in the suit stood by the door and opened it. "Please sir."

Marcus looked at the man in the suit and the doctor and nurse. He then looked at his father. "I'll be right back, dad." He said gently squeezing his dad's hand, standing up and walking out the door that was held open for him.

The doctor, nurse and the man in the suit walked out of the visitors' room, leaving Marcus feeling shocked, dumbfounded and sick with hopelessness and despair. He had tried in vain to argue his father's case but was to no avail. They had told Marcus that unless he can come up with some sort of

112

payment plan they cannot continue treating his father, who was dying of cancer, just because his father's insurance had expired 3 months ago, just before the cancer struck.

The hospital had told Marcus that, although they can no longer treat his father's illness, they will make him comfortable till the end. Meaning they will just pump him full of drugs till he dies. Marcus truly believed his father was covered for his illness. He couldn't afford health insurance for himself, let alone for his father.

Marcus walked out the hospital, tears streaming down his face. He left without saying bye to his father. He couldn't bear to see him after feeling as though he had let him down, the feeling of guilt that he couldn't do anything weighing heavy on his heart.

Marcus pulled up outside his rented home and, having only just stopped crying, exhaled sadly as he opened the car door and stepped out. He opened the gate to his small front garden and walked the path to the front door. The first thing he noticed as he walked through was a black duffel bag by the front door.

"Luciana?" He called out, standing in the hallway.

The door to his right opened and a very beautiful woman, but with a black eye that looked almost fresh, stood in the doorway. She looked frightened. He had met Lucianna 3 years ago in Colombia when he gone travelling alone. The pair quickly fell in love and, after months of phone calls, he returned. He convinced her to take the plunge and move to the states to be with him.

It was about six months later he started showing his true colours.

Marcus frowned. "What is this? What's going on?" he asked, pointing to the bag.

"Shit," she mumbled, fear written all over her face. "I

didn't think you'd be back yet."

Marcus scowled. *"Sorry to disappoint."* he replied, coldly. So, what is with the bag."

Lucianna shakily took a deep breath and walked into the kitchen, taking the time to ready her nerves. Marcus closed the front door and followed right behind her.

"I asked, what is going on? Why is that bag there?" he said with aggression in his slightly raised voice.

"Marcus," Lucianna began saying, her voice quivering. *"I told you. I told you that was the last time you raise your hand at me. I can't stay here anymore. I'm sick of being your punchbag."*

Tears formed suddenly in Marcus's eyes. *"Please, Lucianna, Please don't do this! I know I have been a shitty boyfriend, but I need you right now. I can change, I promise!"* Marcus pleaded. He dropped his head, sighing. *"The hospital are stopping the treatments on my father because of his insurance. Lucianna, without the treatment he only has weeks to live."* Tears began falling down his face.

"God Marcus, I'm sorry," Lucianna spoke softly and placed a hand on his shoulder, squeezing gently. She saw Marcus' father as substitute father of her own since she moved from Colombia.

Marcus raised his hand and placed it on top of hers. Sobbing quietly, tears in full flow.

Despite having genuine sympathy for Marcus, she hadn't changed her mind. She had to get out of this violent relationship.

"I'm sorry Marcus," Lucianna said quietly and slowly. *"But I still have to leave."*

His tears stopped instantly. He slowly lifted his head up and angrily scowled at Lucianna.

"You're still leaving me, even after what I've just told

you?" *His voice sounded sinister.*

"Marcus. I'm sorry about your father, I really am, but I really can't cope anymore. I'm leaving." *Lucianna replied.*

Marcus' angry expression dissolved. "But-but we were trying for a baby!" *he said, desperately.*

"No Marcus, we weren't. I haven't come off the contraception pills."

Marcus frowned. "You lied to me?"

"I had to Marcus. Do you think," *Lucianna was on the verge of tears herself.* "do you seriously think that a baby living in this house with your temperament would be a good thing? You have the worst mood swings, Marcus! I told you before, I really think you have bipolar! One minute you say you love me then literally 10 minutes later you hit me for the slightest reason!"

Tears now fell down Lucianna's face, as all the pent-up anger and frustration erupted. She'd had enough. She decided that the only way she could hurt him back was emotionally. "And there is something else as well you should know seeing as I'm now being honest with you!"

Marcus forced a laugh. "Fuck me. You really are a heartless bitch, aren't you? Go on then." *Marcus folded his arms.*

Lucianna stared at him, instantly regretting saying anything. She had to tell him now though. She hesitated and gulped. "I've been sleeping with someone from work the past 2 months."

Marcus glared at lucianna, remaining quiet and breathing heavily. After a moment of silence, Lucianna turned and picked up her car keys off the counter. "I'm going to go-AAAH!" *she screamed as Marcus flew off his chair, knocking it backwards to the floor as he ran over, wrapping his left hand around her neck and slamming her against the wall, banging her head against it. The car keys fell to the floor as she* gripped her hands around his wrist.

"Marcus! Please, don't!" she pleaded with him, her hands struggling against his.

He squeezed his hand even tighter around her throat, choking her, pinning her in place. He raised his right hand in the air. With as much anger and velocity he could muster, he thrust his fist down. Lucianna screamed as he punched the wall beside her head.

Tears streamed down her face and his hand was still wrapped around her throat. He pulled her face close to his and he shook his head in disgust. He turned to the open kitchen door, dragging her by the neck with him and he pushed as hard as he could, sending her falling backwards and crashing down backwards in the corridor. He picked up her keys and threw them at her, landing on her stomach before hitting the floor.

A week later, almost at midnight. Marcus was on the couch in the den, in a reclined position, head tilted back and fast asleep. His snores drowned out the sound of the TV, the only source of light in the otherwise darkened room. He was dreaming that Lucianna had never left him and that his father was in perfect health. He felt so happy and content that his life was now normal. So idyllic. He was having lunch with both in his kitchen, sat round the circular dining table. Lucianna had made Marcus's favourite Colombian dish, "Bandeja Paisa". He was happily tucking into it, smiling at his father, who was also enjoying the food. There was a phone ringing somewhere. It started off quiet but grew louder with each ring. Much too loud. His father's smile faded, and he looked at Marcus sadly. Something was wrong. He looked from his father towards the lounge, where the ringing was coming from. He then turned and looked back at his father and Lucianna, whose features were starting to fade.

Marcus awoke from his slumber and, opening his eyes, squinted from the glare of the television. He reached up and rubbed the sleep from them with his hands and yawned loudly. He then reached for the remote to switch the TV off. As he pointed the remote at the television he paused, suddenly realising that the ringing wasn't coming from the television set.

The phone on the other side of the lounge was ringing.

Marcus ran over and quickly grabbed the receiver. "Hello?!"

"Marcus, It's Dr. Fints from St. Mary's hospital. I sugg-"

"Is my father okay?" Marcus interrupted, his voice starting to break. "Is he- is he-"

Dr. Fints knew what Marcus was getting at.

"No, Marcus, he is still with us. But for how long I cannot say, probably 3 or 4 hours at most. His breathing has altered to short, shallow breath's. I'm sorry. You should get here as soon as you can."

Marcus slammed the brakes on outside the entrance of the hospital and swung the door open and ran out the car, leaving the door wide open.

"Hey! You can't just leave the car like that! This is for drop offs only! This- HEY!" a hospital orderly shouted as they exited the building and Marcus barged past him, almost knocking him over.

Marcus ran at full speed to the ward where his father had been moved to. A few minutes later he arrived at the entrance of the ward. Marcus placed his hand on the door to push open and stopped.

He was about to say his final goodbye to his father. The only person to have never let him down. Never disappoint him. Never hurt him. Tears formed in his eyes. Marcus fought them down. He steeled himself.

And pushed the door open.

Marcus walked quickly past the closed curtains of the other patients' beds, towards his father's section. He pulled the curtain open to step through. There was a lamp on nearby, and he saw a doctor and a nurse standing on either side of the bed. He couldn't hear what they were saying but the doctor looked at the time and mouthed something to the nurse. They slowly turned to him, looking sombre.

"I'm sorry." The nurse said as she stepped back.

Marcus stumbled past the nurse, towards his deceased father, grief-stricken that he hadn't made it. Tears filled his eyes so much that he couldn't clearly see as he fell by the side of the bed. The nurse and doctor grabbed hold of him for support. Marcus leant over and grabbed his father's lifeless hand and squeezed tightly. He took in a large gulp of air then wailed loudly, the tears pouring down his face.

Marcus' father had set up a funeral package before he passed, albeit a very basic one. The service itself was very small. Next to no-one attended, a few from a club his father attended way back when he was healthy. There wasn't even a reception.

Marcus walked back to his empty house and was about to put the key in the door when there was a cough behind him. Marcus turned around and saw a smartly dressed man standing in the pathway of his house.

"Excuse me, but are you Mr Bovin? I've been waiting for you. I'm Mr Lathams. I'm from "Saxon & Smith Attorneys". Your father dealt with me a few months back, before he was diagnosed." Mr Lathams said. "I'm sorry for your loss, Mr Bovin. Would you mind if I came in? I have some news for *you."*

Once inside, Marcus had made both himself and Mr Lathams a mug of coffee each and Mr Lathams explained that his father had been saving a large portion of his earnings for most of his life and that he also had been paying into a retirement fund since he started work at such a young age. All the remaining monies now belonged to Marcus and because his father died so early into his retirement it meant that it was a substantial amount.

After having such a tough break, his father dying and his bitch of a girlfriend cheating and leaving him, Marcus decided to take a break for 3 months and go back to the only place he felt truly happy: Colombia. Although that was the place he had met and, on his part at least, fell in love with Lucianna, it still held a special place in his heart, and he knew that it would be the best place to cure his heartache. He had taken some time off work and used part of the money left to him by his father.

CHAPTER 21

A few weeks into his vacation, it was late in the evening and Marcus was walking the streets of Medellin. He had made friends with some locals and they had agreed to meet him at a nearby nightclub. Walking past a group of drunk revellers, he guessed the club must be near. Turning the corner on his right, he heard the loud music and saw the flashing lights in the distance. He walked past the bouncers and up to the cashier to pay the entrance fee. Once inside, he walked around the dark, noisy and extremely busy rooms looking for his friends amongst all the people dancing, drinking and smoking. Eventually he found them in a dark corner, huddled together around a circular table.

The three young Colombian locals looked at each other, muttering heatedly, before reluctantly beckoning him over.

"Hey guys! Only just managed to find you!"

Carlos, Oscar and Jhon all nodded, turned back to face each other and began talking quickly amongst themselves.

Feeling slightly uncomfortable, as though he was imposing on a conversation, even though he couldn't hear a word because of the loud music, Marcus asked. "So... you guys want to go get a drink or something?

Oscar turned his head. "Sure Marcus. Go get a drink. We'll see you soon."

Marcus frowned at the bluntness. "you aren't coming? What're you up to?"

This time Carlos turned to him. "Just some business, Marcus. We thought we'd be done by now. Just give us five minutes. Okay?"

Starting to feel pissed off, Marcus shook his head. "I don't give a shit if you're selling drugs. Just don't treat me like a fucking idiot. You guys asked me to meet you here and here I am. Now you want me to fuck off?" he spoke angrily, loud enough for all three Colombians to hear.

Carlos looked at Oscar and Jhon and then back to Marcus. Carlos sighed, and gestured for Marcus to come closer. "Fine Marcus. Just keep fucking quiet about whatever -whatever- you see tonight. Okay? Someone has asked us to deliver something to them. We just have to find it first."

For the next half hour, they hardly spoke, just looking at all the partygoers on the dance floor and spoke quietly to each other. Then Carlos pointed to two girls on the dance floor.

They each had drinks in their hands, and they walked off the dance floor towards the ladies bathroom. They placed their drinks on a vacant table nearby and pushed the bathroom door open and walked through. Jhon quickly handed something to Oscar under the table.

"Remember. You don't say a fucking thing." Carlos said hurriedly to Marcus, as Jhon quickly walked over towards the drinks and emptied a sachet into one of them, picking it up and rapidly but gently swirling it in his hands, ensuring whatever he had emptied into the drink had all dissolved, before placing it back in its precise location and speedily walked back to the others. A second later the two girls had stumbled out of the door, laughing and giggling. They drunkenly wobbled over to the table, picked up the drinks and went back to the dance floor. Carlos checked the time on his wristwatch.

"What was that stuff?" Marcus asked quietly, even though by the noise of the club no one would have heard him

if he had yelled.

Carlos, Oscar and Jhon all looked at each other.

They explained that, in Colombia, there is a drug that takes away peoples free will, and most of the people who have heard about it all think it is a story made up to warn tourists and backpackers of the dangers of being drugged; it is a myth and not to be believed.

After twenty minutes, Carlos checked his watch.

"It's time."

Carlos moved from the small table they were gathered around and danced across the dark, crowded dance floor. Because of the flashing strobe lights and the smoke machine it made it hard to see clearly but eventually he found the two girls. One was dancing on a podium, completely unaware her friend was drugged. The other was standing next to it, hardly moving. Carlos approached her from behind and he began gyrating his hips against her backside. He leant forward and spoke in her ear. Then he backed away, slowly making his way across the floor dancing with other women.

A minute later, the girl walked from the dance floor and towards the exit, her friend never noticed and danced away, oblivious that she was never going to see her friend again.

Once she had disappeared out the building, Oscar and Jhon followed close behind her.

Left alone at the Table, Marcus was dumbfounded at what he had just witnessed. He had heard of this drug before, but like many others, thought it was just a myth, a fable to scare unsuspecting travellers.

Carlos was walking back to the table.

"What's going to happen to her? To the girl?" Marcus asked Carlos.

Carlos smirked cruelly. "We'll contact a few people. There are always people looking to buy organs on the black market."

Marcus' mouth fell wide open at what Carlos had said. "But-But what about the police? Won't they go looking for her?"

"They might make a bit of an effort if it was a local girl. But a traveller," he waved his hand. "they won't do a thing. For all they know, she may have gotten pissed off with her friend and decided to move on to the next part of their journey alone."

In the room of the shabby hotel he was staying in, Marcus read all the local papers and watched the local news for two weeks after the incident. There wasn't one word concerning the girl.

Marcus had become fascinated that where was a drug that could do that to a person, to completely lose self-control and become helpless, vulnerable and at the mercy of someone else. He researched it more and more throughout his time in Colombia. Only witnessing two more times what the effects of this drug can do to a person, each time in a different club.

Marcus had stayed for a month longer than originally planned. He felt he had nothing to return to the States for. No girlfriend. No family. Why the hell not he thought. His work won't exactly miss him.

When he did return home, he opened the door and picked the mountain of bills up off the floor and placed them on the table next to the door. He could hear the beeps of the answering machine, telling him that, as well as the letters, there was also a mountain of messages for him. Every message was regarding some sort of debt.

And so it starts, he sighed to himself

A few days later, Marcus walked into his work and was

immediately summoned up to the office by his boss.

"Get your stuff together and get out." Carl, his boss, said abruptly.

Marcus stood, shocked. "Wait! What? I- don't understand!"

"Marcus, you had unauthorised absence! It was bad enough that you had two months off at the drop of a hat but to have another month off without notifying us?! That is a sackable offence." Carl smugly replied, leaning back in his chair behind his desk.

"Look, Carl, please don't do this! I need this job! Please! I thought it would be okay if I just had one more month out there. Considering what I've been through." He pleaded with his boss.

"Marcus," Carl sighed. "I ran out of sympathy for you a hell of a long time ago. It's done. You are done. Get your stuff and get the hell out. Now." he said angrily, not moving from his desk.

Marcus began breathing heavily, his heart was thumping. Fury erupted within Marcus. He knew that no matter what he said, it wouldn't make a difference. Breathing heavily, he looked at his now-former boss. "You fucking dick."

Carl looked surprised by Marcus. "What did you just say?" he asked, furiously.

"You heard me," Marcus said quietly, walking slowly towards the desk. "You are nothing more than a fucking dick. All you do all day is make people feel like shit and worthless, bullying them whenever you can to make yourself feel important, but then make out to be best friends with them when the bigger dicks above you are around," Marcus chuckled as he placed both hands on the desk and leaned forward. "but you can't fucking bully me anymore. You better hope I don't see you in the streets." He whispered, menacingly.

Carl gulped and momentarily looked taken aback, unsure of how to react. Then his face screwed up and the colour of his face changed to an angry red hue.

"What the hell is that supposed to mean?!" he yelled, an angry vein on his bald head clearly visible.

"It means I will fucking slaughter you." Marcus coldly replied. Standing up and turning to the door. He grabbed the handle and, opening it, he looked at his former boss.

"Have a good day, Carl."

Marcus walked out of the building with nearly the same feeling he had when his father had died. Lost. Angry. Distraught. Disappointed. Furious.

Outside his front door, key in hand, Marcus had no recollection of the journey home. Surely things couldn't get much worse. Could they? He felt like he was almost at rock bottom. Bad things after bad things seemed to keep happening to him.

No. No. He wasn't going to be beaten. Sure, he had just lost his job, but in truth he didn't care much for it anyway. He still had enough cash left over from his father to see him by till he found a new job.

His father. That wound won't ever heal. The one person to be there for him. To raise him since his mom had walked out when he was in his early teens and never returned. His father never liked to talk about her. Only ever said that she wasn't happy for a long time before she left.

As for Lucianna, He didn't need that negative slut in his life anyway.

No. He will not be beaten.

Opening his front door, he saw a letter on the doormat. Bending down to pick it up he noticed it said URGENT on the front of it, above the address. Sighing to himself, he closed the door and walked down the hall towards the living room and torn open the letter.

Boom. Rock bottom had been hit.

The letter stated that, with deep regret, he was to be evicted from the premises within the next 4 weeks. The Landord is selling the property.

Marcus stared at the letter clutched in his hand. His whole life was falling apart.

Within months, he had lost everything.

He had never such anger and fury. He screamed as loudly as he could, swung round and delivered a series of kicks and punches to whatever was in close proximity to him, causing as much damage as possible. The wall. The door. The table in the hallway. After a minute of punching, kicking and screaming, he stopped and inhaled deeply. Then he assessed the damage around him. The table had a leg kicked off during the outburst and lay up-ended. The mirror above smashed and pieces of glass lay scattered on the floor. The door was hanging off by its hinges. The plasterboard wall on the opposite side had a whole punched through it.

He took another deep breath and decided. Enough.

That night, he had an idea and put his plans in motion.

CHAPTER 22

Detective Cross and Shaw sat opposite each other, both leaning on the table. The only difference was that Shaw was handcuffed to the table.

"I've already told you. If you want Marcus, then you can have his number! Its-Its on my phone!" Shaw nervously mumbled.

"No Lee…. Well yes, we do want to find this Marcus. But no, You aren't gonna get out of it that easily."

Shaw frowned. "I-I just gave you his name *and* I'm giving you his number! What more do you fucking want?!"

James's smile disappeared. "You are going to help us bring him in, Lee. And watch your language please."

Shaw gawked at James like a deer caught in the headlights. "Help you bring him in? How?" he asked uneasily.

Ten minutes later James sat on the corner of the table and placed Shaw's cell phone in front of him. Lee looked at the phone then up at James, who was sat on the edge of the table.

"You're going to call Marcus and arrange to meet him." Shaw gasped in objection. Detective Cross raised his hand. "Don't worry, you will be wearing a wire and we will be literally 20 seconds away from you. You'll be perfectly safe." He added, noting the colour draining from Shaw's face within seconds.

"Are you kidding me?!" Shaw blurted out. "He-He'll fucking kill me!"

James shook his head. "No Lee. He won't get chance to. Like I said, we will only be a few seconds away from you both. We just want you to meet up with him, then as soon as we see him with this substance, we'll move in."

"Isn't that called entrapment?"

James looked surprised by this and shook his head. "No, not in cases like this. It just makes things easier for us when said suspect is caught in the act. Makes things run a hell of a lot smoother on our side. So," James moved the phone closer to Shaw. "Make the call Lee."

Shaw sighed and picked up the phone. Unlocking it, he found the required contact number. He had it stored under a false name. He hesitated when it came to pressing dial.

"What's the matter Lee?" James asked.

"What if something goes wrong? I-I don't know if I can do this." Shaw started hyperventilating heavily and dropped the phone back down on the table. James placed a hand on his shoulder.

"I understand you're nervous. But I *guarantee* that if you don't pick up that phone and make the call, you will be spending a hell of lot longer in prison than you would do if you did make the call." James removed his hand from Shaw's shoulder. "Tell you what, if this doesn't work, then we will still treat you as a co-operative and the offer will still stand."

Shaw shakily picked up the phone, found the required contact number once more and hit dial.

CHAPTER 23

Sitting nervously in the back of the unmarked police people carrier, Shaw was facing Detective James Cross, who was fitting him up with a wire. James concealed the microphone under the zipper of Shaws's hooded jacket.

"Won't he see this?" Shaw asked.

James shook his head, "No he won't. Don't worry. It'll be well hidden. We've done this hundreds of times. No one ever see's the wire. What they *do* notice, however," James said, handing Shaw some paper towels, "is how nervous the person *wearing* the wire is. You need to calm down, Lee. Just breathe slowly and wipe your face, you're covered in sweat." Lee took the towels and patted it on his face, wiping away the perspiration.

"You've got ten minutes before the meeting. We're going to drop you off here and you can walk to the meeting point. We'll drive there now and so will the other vehicles. And, just in case you have any bright ideas," James added. "one'll remain here and follow you, just to make sure you don't do a Speedy Gonzales and do a runner on us."

Shaw looked momentarily confused by the last part of what James said, clearly too young to remember the Looney Tunes character, but nevertheless, he understood what James was saying. "Don't worry. I won't run. I just want this over with." he said.

"Attaboy," James smiled. "so do we. Soon as we have Marcus in custody it'll be over. So then, we'll see and hear you at the meeting point. Good luck." With that James leant across and opened the door for Shaw to exit the vehicle.

Alone now in the street, save for the one remaining unmarked police car, Shaw started walking to the meeting point. He had tried to sound as casual as he could on the phone to Marcus. He had made out that he had used his bag of Devils Breath and he needed some more. Marcus seemed to have bought it and they had arranged to meet outside a garage, in a street that is hardly ever used apart from hookers and drug dealers. Now though however, it was empty. Hearing the vehicle's engine start up behind him and follow him as he walked down the street, Shaw made his way the destination, trying to look as casual as possible. He took deep, steady breaths, attempting to calm his fast-beating heart.

Everything'll be ok. It'll be over in an hour, he kept repeating in is head.

Standing now outside the meeting point, Shaw kept glancing at the unmarked police vehicles, double-*double* checking that they were there, and that they could clearly hear him by coughing and discreetly gesturing to them.

Watching through binoculars, James gritted his teeth in frustration. "For God's sake, He's gonna give himself away!" although they could clearly hear Lee, he could not hear them as it wasn't a two-way radio.

Satisfied that he wasn't alone and, therefore safe, Shaw turned his attention back to the meeting. He looked at his wristwatch. Two minutes to go. *Anytime now*, he took in a huge lungful of air and tried to calm his nerves.

Ten minutes had passed, which added to Shaw's stress and anxiety. He tried his hardest to hide this feeling but couldn't help glancing nervously at the vehicles. Every time he did, James became more agitated. *Stop looking! For God's sake!*

After a further ten minutes had passed. Sweat now covered Shaw's face, he was breathing so heavily, he thought his heart was going to thump out of his chest. Looking quickly from one vehicle to the next, not knowing what to do, he was panicking more than ever. He had not been briefed what to do in case this - *a no show* - happened. Glancing once more around the empty street and unoccupied high-rise buildings surrounding him, he decided what to do.

Shaw lifted the hidden microphone up to his mouth, "Hey guys, wha-"

It happened in a split second.

Shaw's head was blown off completely, his limp body fell to the ground in a crumpled heap, blood spurting out from his neck, where his head had once been.

"FUCK!" James screamed out.

A cop jumped out of one of the vehicles. He was immediately shot in the back. Two more cops were running on the opposite side and they too were shot. One in the stomach and the other in the neck.

"SHIT! Officers down, officers down!" Detective Cross frantically yelled into the radio, still in the car, scanning the surrounding buildings looking for the shooter.

From his vantage point on top of the building, Marcus knew he couldn't keep firing all day and had to move quickly. He took a few more pot-shots at the police. Satisfied that they were either now dead or running for cover, he moved down from where he was kneeling and unscrewed the telescopic rifle into three parts and placed them in the cushioned case. He had bought the rifle illegally, as he did with all his guns, with the money from his father's insurance. It had no registered name to it so didn't matter whether it was left it at the scene, he had ensured to only ever handle it with latex gloves so there were no fingerprints on it but nevertheless still wanted to keep it. He closed the casing, picked it up by the handle and ran as fast as he could to the stairwell at back of the building. He had only a matter of time before the police figured out where the shots were coming from.

When Marcus got the call off Shaw, he had a gut feeling that the police were now involved. He had arranged to meet with him to find out for sure. He could've walked away without firing, but as soon as he saw Shaw speak into the hidden microphone, he felt such anger and betrayal that he couldn't help himself. He knew that now it would only be a matter of time before the police find him now, but Shaw had to pay for his disloyalty.

Marcus sprinted down the stairwell at full speed, jumping down the steps four at a time. He was at the bottom within minutes and could hear the approaching sirens in the distance. At the footwell of the stairwell, he creaked open the door and peered through. There were no police down this side street yet so he moved out as quickly and quietly as he could. He was almost at the end of the side street when he heard a cop approaching around the corner. Crouching and ducking behind a nearby dumpster, the cop continued past him down the side street. Marcus exhaled quietly, creeping up from his stooped position and made his way to the end of the side street.

"FREEZE!"

Marcus stopped, dropping the rifle case with a loud thud and raised his hands. *Shit!* He turned and saw that the cop had his gun raised and pointed at his chest. "You're the one, aren't you?! You're the one who fired at us!" The cop yelled, his hands unshaking. Marcus remained silent with his hands in the air. "On your knees and interlock your fingers! Now!" the cop shouted. Marcus knelt on his knees and placed his hands on his head. Slowly the cop moved forward, the gun still pointed at Marcus with one hand as his other reached for the handcuffs attached to his belt. The cop stood behind Marcus, reading the Miranda rights to him. "You have the right to remain silent. If you give up the right to remain silent, anything you say can and will be used against you in a court of law." The cop lowered the gun whilst reading Marcus his rights, placing the first handcuff around Marcus' left wrist. "You have the right to an attorney. If you-"

Before the cop could finish reading the rights, with as much strength as he could muster, Marcus yanked his right elbow back, snapping the cops kneecap backwards, instantly shattering it. Marcus got on his feet. Screaming in agony, the cop fell to the floor, writhing in pain. The gun fell beside him. The officer grabbed the gun and as he went to point it at him, Marcus kicked his hand, causing the gun to misfire at a wall before flying out of his grip. The cop screamed once more and reached his other hand reached for the radio. He frantically brought the radio up to his mouth and pressed the button to radio for help but before he could speak Marcus bought up his foot and stamped as hard as he could on the cop's throat, crushing his larynx. Choking to death, spluttering vast amounts of blood, he dropped his radio. Marcus stamped again, bursting his neck open, killing him instantly.

Detective Cross and the one officer who hadn't been shot had separated to find the shooter before he escaped. They both decided that they couldn't wait for the backup. Detective Cross held his gun out in front of him, searching the empty streets when he heard the gunshot. The same feeling of dread that he had had when Kelly had been hit by the car had washed over him again. He ran as fast as he could towards where the sound of the gunshot had come from. He ran down the side street and turned the corner and saw the body on the floor, covered in blood where his throat had once been.

The view in front of him paralyzed James. He couldn't move or speak. The brutality that had befallen the officer had shook him to his core. He reached for his radio.

"Officer down." He spoke quietly into it, still in shock. "I'm sorry. My god, I'm sorry. This was my fault." he started weeping. He fell to his knees, beside the body.

James didn't see the figure approaching quietly from behind.

Marcus raised the concrete slab he had found behind the dumpster and swung down as hard as he could, sending James's world black.

CHAPTER 24

The headache nearly split his head open. James groaned as he opened his eyes. Everything was a blur. He closed his eyes and dropped his head, trying to remember what happened.

Lee. A sting operation gone awry. Death. Lots of death.

James slowly opened his eyes and blinked. One. Two. Three times.

He lifted his head and looked around the empty, dank area. His eyes began to focus and adjust to the darkness of the room. It was dirty, damp and empty, apart from a stool in the corner next to the door. He went to rub his forehead but couldn't. It was then he noticed his left arm was handcuffed to a rusty disused pipe against a wall, and he was slumped awkwardly on the dirty floor. He tried to stand up, but the movement of his body caused his headache to flare up tenfold. He crumpled to the floor moaning.

"Ah, you're awake! Finally!" a voice said.

James looked up. He hadn't seen the man walk through the door at the far end of the dark room.

"Who are you?" James asked, wincing in pain as he spoke. He took a moment for the pain to subside. "Where am I?" he murmured.

Marcus made a look of mock indignation. "*Who* am I?

Really?" he said smirking, then his tone changed darker. "You know *exactly* who I am. I'm assuming it was your idea that turned to shit out there. As for where you are, you're in an abandoned building in "The Tenderloin". Luckily, I managed to get you here before your buddies arrived."

James dropped his head. "You must be Marcus." He sighed.

Marcus started clapping. "Well done! Really well done!" he replied, "No wonder they made you Detective."

James frowned and looked up, "How do you-" he began to ask.

"We'll get to that soon, Detective Cross."

James dropped his head again and exhaled. "Okay. Then maybe you can tell me why; Why are you doing all of this? Why are you keeping me here in this room? Why didn't you just kill me, like you've killed everyone else?"

Marcus picked up the old wooden stool and placed it across from James, leaning forward, facing him. "So many questions. Okay, I'll answer your first question first. *Why* am I doing this? Well, like all good stories, I might as well start at the beginning; Firstly, my mother left me when I was at a tender age…"

James dropped his head again, sighing loudly. "Classic. A psychopath with mommy issues."

Marcus scowled at this comment. "Pay attention, Detective Cross. You're going to want to listen to me. I assure you." Marcus said in a threatening tone. "Like I said, my mother left when I was young, leaving my father to bring me up. He done his best, but I didn't have the happiest upbringing most kids have. I got the shit beat outta me at school on a daily basis. It was then my dad really taught me some valuable lessons. He taught me to fight back. Fight back hard. Eventually they learnt that they were messing with the wrong kid. But you know what? I actually *enjoyed* fighting back. The look on their faces when I smashed one of their faces up that bad, I knocked some teeth out. Man, that gave me a such a rush.

My father was also an expert marksman. He used to take me to gun ranges, where he practised. He passed his skills onto me, teaching me all about guns and how to use them. When I wasn't practising with him at the ranges, I used to practice on small animals. Birds. Cats. Even dogs. I didn't always kill them though, just wing them. Aim for a leg or two sometimes. It was so funny watching them writhe around in pain." Marcus had a vacant look as he reminisced, smiling fondly at the thoughts. "I eventually learned that my dad was the saviour in my life. And so, I finished school and found a job. I saved up enough money to go travelling. *See the world before it's too late* as my dad used to say. To cut a long story short, I *did* go travelling and I fell in love with a beautiful Colombian woman, Lucianna. Finally, my life looked like it was on the up. She eventually agreed to move here and start a new life with me. We even talked about having a baby." Marcus said this last part bitterly, with a sad smile on his face.

"But, then my father became ill. Cancer. Terminal. There was nothing the doctors could do. Or should I say, there is nothing the doctors *would* do," his tone became angry now. "Just because my father's goddamn insurance had expired, they refused to treat him any longer! Just let him die! Is-is that even legal?! I mean, can they do that?!" his voice became aggressive.

James wasn't sure whether he was supposed to answer, so he just remained quiet.

"Anyway, whilst my dad was dying in that shit excuse

of a hospital, my girlfriend decides to tell me she's leaving me, that she never truly wanted a baby with me *and* that she's been fucking another guy!"

James noticed that the more Marcus talked, the angrier and crazy eyed he became.

"So, that bitch leaves me and then my father died! *If only* he had the sense to renew his fucking insurance before he became sick!" Marcus was breathing heavily now.

"I gave my father a modest funeral," He said softly, trying to calm himself. "Then afterwards I find out my dad had left a shit ton of money for me. Why the *fuck* didn't he just take out the health insurance instead?!" His eyes filled with tears.

"I used some of the cash to go travelling again. To clear my head after all the shit. It was then I discovered *Devils Breath*. I'm not gonna go into details, but I was amazed by it. How this drug can take away peoples free will and do whatever they were told to do, is extraordinary. *To become God.*

I came back after a while, ready to take on the world.

I returned to work, only to be immediately told that I had unauthorised absence and was being sacked immediately." Marcus said quietly, staring at an uninteresting spot on the ground, lost in thought. "I walked out of there, wondering, *why*? Why me? My life seems to be a constant state of misery. *Here*," he gestured to the floor. "When I'm away, out of San Francisco, I have a normal, happy life with no unexpected, unwanted surprises. But here!" he gestured to the floor again. "I tried not to let that beat me. I was determined not to let that beat me. And then when I got home, I found a letter telling me that I was becoming homeless."

James expected Marcus to get angry again but instead

he started laughing.

"It was then I decided that enough is enough. I was sick of my life. I was going to take control-"

"Take control by killing people?" James interrupted.

"No! Take control by bringing it here! No more taking shit off people! Instead I would be the one dishing it out. I could be *God*. As I started looking for alternative accommodation, I realised that buildings like this were being sold for less than a third of a price of a house. So, using my father's name and my mother's maiden name, I purchased this place. I mean, why not? It has running water, and electricity in *most* of the rooms." Marcus looked like a crazy person, wide eyed and laughing manically.

James kept his voice calm. "So, you brought this drug here to, what? frighten people?"

"Yes. Frighten," Marcus replied. "and gain respect."

"Respect?!" James chuckled, "It still doesn't make any sense to me. You've just saw something in Colombia and wanted to copy it. You're no different to any other-"

"I am completely different!" Marcus yelled, standing up quickly and knocking the stool over. "Yes, I saw this drug in Colombia, but I didn't just copy it! I *improved* it! Ever since my first subject I have worked tirelessly on improving its effect more and more!"

James spat on the floor and looked at Marcus in the eyes. "Your first subject? You mean Tim Allwood at the bank? Why *did* you want his money anyway? Why did you want *any* money if you already had a *shit ton* from your father?"

Marcus took a deep breath. "I didn't want his money. I didn't *need* any money. It was never about that. It was just a test. That's all."

James snapped. "That man had a family!"

"Look, I didn't have time to do research into his background. Anyway," Marcus said, quietly. "I never said he was my first subject."

James looked up at Marcus.

"My first subject was Sean Connor."

CHAPTER 25

Sean Conner and Jennifer Reilly were sat opposite each other in McCoys Irish bar.

"Are you sure we've got enough time for this? I should be there soon!" Jennifer asked, worriedly.

"Babe, relax. We've got plenty of time. It's not that busy in here, so service should be quick enough. We'll just have a quick bite to eat, then head off again! Don't worry!" Sean said, grabbing hold of her hand. Jennifer looked at the watch on her other wrist.

"I know, I'm just a bit stressed about it." She said, laughing nervously.

"You'll be fine! Besides, you will need a full stomach to calm yourself! No point in going for an audition starving hungry and forgetting your lines!"

Jennifer was an enthusiastic-but-so-far-unsuccessful actress. She had an audition for a play, and word was that a former Hollywood celebrity was due to star in it.

If she nailed this, then who knows what could happen afterwards.

"Okay, okay!" she relented, smiling.

After they had eaten, they gestured to the waitress for the bill.

"I'm so nervous! I feel like I'm going to throw my salad back up!" Jennifer said, anxiously.

"You. Will. Be. Fine!" Sean said reassuringly. "Look, go

to the bathroom and wash your face. Take a few minutes to calm yourself and then we will be on our way, where you will smash this audition."

Jennifer's eyes filled with tears, not because she was worried about her audition, but for her love for Sean. He really was her rock. She leant forward over the table and kissed him.

"I love you." She said.

"I love you too. Now go wash your face, while I go pay. Christ knows where this waitress is." He replied as they both stood up from the table. Neither could see the figure out in the car park watching them.

They exited the bar together and walked over to Sean's car. Sean pressed the UNLOCK button on his key fob as they approached it. The car didn't flash its headlights to confirm it was now unlocked, meaning only one thing.

"Didn't you lock it?" Jennifer asked.

Sean frowned, "I thought I did." he replied.

"Sean, you can't afford to have this car stolen! You have to be careful!" she said.

"I know! It was just a mistake, that's all!" Sean muttered, rolling his eyes. "Come on, let's get you to that audition" he said, hoping to change the subject.

They both opened their doors and got in the car, Sean in the driver's seat and Jennifer in the passenger. In unison, they both closed the doors. Sean reached for the key, inserted it into the ignition and turned it.

Immediately, when the engine turned on and the interior fan kicked in, a cloudy puff of particles shot out of the fans and spread throughout the car.

Both Sean and Jennifer coughed for a few seconds, confused.

"What the he-" Sean began to say, before falling silent.

The feeling of helplessness that washed over them both was unbearable. They couldn't move or talk. They just sat still, wondering what the hell was happening to them.

A door to the back seat of the car opened, and a man, wearing a full jacket, latex gloves and a face mask climbed in the backseat, and closed the door.

"Hello you two." The man began saying. "Firstly, let me apologise about this. It was only because Romeo here didn't lock his car that I chose you two. Had he done, then I would've had to carry on waiting for someone else to leave their vehicle unlocked." Sean and Jennifer sat still, unmoving but completely aware of this unwelcome visitor. "Secondly, what you are experiencing is completely normal. It is a drug that I find completely fascinating and, hopefully, improved. By the looks of you two, it has." Marcus said, proudly. "Although unfortunately, for you pair, this isn't where the trial ends. On average, it takes 37 minutes to drive through the centre of San Francisco, I want you to do it in 20 minutes. No particular reason, just because, really. And to make things a bit more interesting, just in case the police manage to stop you, I want you to drink this, between you both." He reached into his jacket and pulled out a bottle of vodka. Reaching for the door handle, he turned and said. "Good luck guys! Remember, drink ALL of the bottle first."

He exited the car and made his way across the street to his own vehicle. Sean slowly reached for the vodka and unscrewed the cap. He raised the bottle to his lips and tipped the contents down his throat, gulping down large mouthfuls, gagging as the vodka burnt his insides. He only lowered it when the bottle was half empty. He then handed it to Jennifer, who took it off him and copied what Sean had done. Once the bottle was empty, she dropped it on the car floor. Sean shifted the car into gear, drove out of the car park and towards the city. The roads were pretty clear. Any cars that were on the road, they bypassed without incident. The speedometer crept higher and higher as they got closer to the city. By the time they had entered the city they were creeping just up to 90mph. People had to dive out of the way or slam on their brakes as Sean sped past them.

Although they were sat in silence, their eyes filled with tears as they couldn't stop themselves. All they wanted to do was slam on the brakes and hold each other. Outside became a blur. They were fast approaching an intersection. They sped across it at full speed, narrowly avoiding a truck on their right. Further down the road, ahead of them was a pedestrian crossing, with only one car in front. Sean pulled the steering wheel to the left to bypass it. A heavily pregnant woman walking on the crossing had just walked out in front. Sean had seen her but was unable to brake, only accelerate even more. Tears were now streaming down Sean and Jennifer's faces. A sickening thud as the car hit her, throwing her into the air then hitting the windscreen, cracking and smearing it with blood. Her lifeless body fell to the floor immediately afterwards. The car still didn't stop. No longer being able to see where they were heading, the car veered to the right. Neither of them was wearing a belt as they didn't buckle up before the Devils Breath affected them. The airbags failed to open as the vehicle hit the building in front of them. The impact of the crash killing Sean and Jennifer instantly.

CHAPTER 26

James was breathing heavily. He felt like he was going to throw up. He was struggling to comprehend everything Marcus had just said. This was the man responsible for Kelly and his unborn baby's death. He tried to speak but couldn't find the words. He began hyperventilating.

James looked up at Marcus, hatred in his eyes. "Y-Y-You...She's...Beca-" he began to stutter. He awkwardly stood up. The handcuff attached to his left arm rattled up the rusty disused gas pipe with him.

Marcus sighed. "I recognised you immediately from the report in the papers a few days later."

James started sobbing, shaking his head, breathing heavily.

Marcus went to speak again, "I-"

"YOU FUCKING KILLED HER!" James lunged for Marcus with his free right arm, his hand swung at Marcus. Marcus stepped back just in time.

Marcus wasn't surprised by this outburst, "I never inte-"

"MY WIFE AND BABY ARE DEAD BECAUSE OF YOU!" James screamed, wild eyes fixed on Marcus. He was still lunging at Marcus.

Marcus calmly took a breath. "Yes, but I never-"

"I'M GONNA FUCKING KILL YOU! YOU FUCKING FUCK, I SWEAR I'M GONNA RIP YOUR GODDAMN

HEARTOUT, YOU PIECE OF SHIT!" James screamed, so loud he thought he was going to tear his vocal cords. He started yanking his secured arm, causing the unused gas pipe to shake whenever he did.

Marcus now spoke loudly back at him. "No, Detective Cross. I didn't kill her, Sean Connor did. He was the one who drove into her, killing her. But yes, he was under the effect of *my* drug at the time. It was never my intention for your wife, or baby, to die, Detective Cross." he sighed.

James was now more like a chained wild dog, alternating between lunging out viciously for Marcus and yanking at his free arm. Even the snarling noises he made resembled an animal intent on ripping apart its closest victim.

Slowly, Detective Cross stopped reaching out for Marcus and eventually stopped pulling at the handcuff, realising that it was useless. He was still, however, still reeling with such anger and adrenaline that he was shaking throughout his whole body.

"Like I said, I recognised you immediately from the tabloids article." Marcus calmly repeated, now James had quietened down. Marcus reached down and picked up the wooden stool he had knocked over, setting it down beside the wall near the door he had walked through. He then stood again in front, but just out of reach, of James.

"That is why I didn't kill you earlier.... I was going to. Believe me I was going to. But then I saw you. It was as though it was some divine fate, or something, that brought us together, Detective Cross. Don't get me wrong, I still mean to kill you. And I will. But you can't deny that fate bought us together. I knew I had to tell you the truth before I killed you.

After I knocked you out, I found the handcuff key on the cop's body. I had to move quick though, I could hear your buddies coming literally minutes away." Marcus smiled saying this. "Glad I decided to keep the handcuffs! Came in useful! Don't you think?"

James didn't acknowledge anything that Marcus had just said. He just stared at him with hatred.

"Detective Cross, I would really like it if you talked to me." Marcus said, "Talk, Not shout." He added.

For a moment James just glared. Then he spoke quietly, although the venom in his voice was still present. "You took away my family. You killed my wife and my baby. I never even got to *hold* my baby." His voice cracked and his eyes filled with tears again.

Marcus sighed, although this time it was more with irritation. "Sean killed your wife, Detective Cross. He drove into her. Not me. I never told him to *aim* for her."

"It *was* you. You *and* your goddamn drug killed my Kelly, and my baby." James started crying again, "And you killed Sean and his girlfriend!" for the first time ever, James felt sorrow, not anger, towards Sean and Jennifer.

Marcus rolled his eyes. "My *goddamn* drug is so good that you, or your buddies, didn't even know that Sean and Jennifer were drugged. You, and everyone else," Marcus said through gritted teeth, pointing at James. "believed that they were drunk. That itself proves how good my drug is. And it – as well as I - should be respected." Marcus paused for a moment, before adding in a sinister tone, "And if it's any comfort to you, you will be joining your family right now." He reached behind him and took out a pistol he had tucked down the back of his pants. He pointed the gun at James' face.

Detective Cross stared back defiantly. He wouldn't

give Marcus the satisfaction of looking away, appearing to be scared.

A banging noise came from the closed door that Marcus had walked through. Marcus, gun still aimed at James, looked back towards the door.

More banging. It was coming from a room further down.

Marcus looked back at James. "Better go see what the noise is first, huh?" he said, grinning, lowering the weapon. "You lucky bastard, saved by the bell. For now. Don't worry though, I won't be long."

He turned on the spot and walked out of the room, closing the door behind him. James had inhaled deeply as soon as Marcus aimed the gun at him. In after what felt like forever, he let out a huge breath. He stood alone in the room, shaking, either from adrenaline or fear, he wasn't sure. But he knew he had to escape somehow. He looked around the room for some inspiration to enable him to accomplish this task.

None came. It was impossible.

He fell to the floor, feeling hopeless. "I'm sorry Kelly." He whimpered quietly, wrapping both his hands around the pipe and closed his eyes.

Another bang. And shouting this time. Although it didn't sound English.

The loud and unexpected noise caused James to jolt from his peaceful acceptance. The sudden movement caused the pipe to shake again. James felt the vibration in his hands, still wrapped around the pipe. He opened his eyes and looked at his hands. Near the bottom of the pipe, just below his hands, it bent and curved into the wall. He gripped tighter and shook them again. With more strength, he clutched the pipe and pushed and pulled the part that turned into the wall. He positioned his feet against the wall, gripped the pipe, pushed his feet and pulled his hands as hard as he could. The was cracking sound. Not a very loud one, but a cracking sound, nonetheless. He checked the pipe and, sure enough, there was the tiniest crack where the rusty pipe had split apart.

CHAPTER 27

Marcus walked out of the room into a smaller corridor, and through another door that led into a larger corridor. The corridor itself was like almost every other room in the building, dark, dirty and damp. All the windows on his right were filthy and grubby. They hadn't been cleaned in decades; some were even cracked. On his left were a series of doors reaching the entire length of the corridor. He walked up to the first door and unlocked it with a key in his pocket. As he turned the handle and pushed it there were a commotion coming from inside.

Stepping into the room was like stepping into an entirely different building. Whereas the rest of the building was dark, dirty and musty; this room was extremely sterile and immaculate. There were cupboards lined on the walls and a large metallic table in the middle of the room. On the table were several trays lined up neatly and accordingly in a row, and there were cutting utensils and measuring scales next to each tray. Marcus had trained each chemist exactly how to weigh, cut, crush, grind and mix each drug, in a meticulous sequence, to make his version of *Devils Breath*. Each tray was labelled up with the required drug of which should be in that particular area tray. At the back of the row, behind all the other trays, was a tray that contained the desired result, *Devils Breath*, with just a blank label in front of it.

Marcus walked in and saw his three Mexican chemists clearly in the middle of a heated argument. They had broken out into a disagreement when Jorge and Hector started speaking of confronting Marcus about being held captive. Roberto, although he relished the idea of standing up to Marcus, feared the outcome. He was still in vast amounts of pain, and remembered clearly about what Marcus said, about punishing their families.

"Caballeros, ¿por qué todo el ruido?" Marcus asked angrily.

Gentlemen, why all the noise?

All three of the chemists looked terrified and fell silent at the unexpected intrusion. They looked at each other, unsure of what to say. Hector took a deep breath and began to speak but was interrupted by Jorge and Roberto. They all raised their voices, trying to be heard, in a muddled mix of English and Spanish. Marcus frowned and sighed, beginning to feel irritated. He couldn't make out a single word.

Hector, Jorge and Roberto were standing opposite Marcus yelling, gesturing alternately at each other, then the window, then the door, then at the table where they made Devils Breath for Marcus.

Marcus frowned and reached up to pinch the bridge of his nose, feeling the onset of a migraine if this carried on.

"Shut up." Marcus said.

Still, they continued shouting at him.

"Shut up." he repeated, growing more incensed. Yet, the chemists still were shouting, louder than ever. It was then he realised that his chemists were at the end of their limits and weren't going to follow his orders anymore.

"WILL YOU SHUT THE FUCK UP!" Marcus yelled,

reached for his gun, pointing it at Roberto and shot him in the head. He turned the gun at Hector.

"¡No! ¡Señor! ¡Por favor!" Hector screamed, hands sprawled out in front of him. Marcus shot him twice in his chest. He fell to the ground dead.

Jorge, his head bowed, started weeping. Marcus pointed the gun at him. Jorge then slowly looked up at Marcus with watery eyes.

"Nunca nos ibas a dejar ir, ¿verdad?" Jorge said, despairingly.

You were never just going to let us leave, were you?

Marcus shook his head, "No, I'm afraid I wasn't.".

Tears ran down Jorge's face, "What about our families?" he mumbled in broken English, his voice shaking at the realisation that he was about to die. Gun still aimed at Jorge, Marcus shrugged his shoulders, "I won't harm them. But they won't ever see you again." he said coldly and pulled the trigger.

Standing in the room with the three dead chemists, Marcus knew it was coming to an end for him, one way or another. It was just a matter of time. He pulled his phone out of his pocket and called his four remaining dealers. He had previously told them all to stay together and out of sight.

Oakley answered on the fourth ring.

"Oakley, put me on loud-speaker for the others to hear,"

There was a clicking sound on the receiver as Oakley done as he was told.

"Shoot" Oakley said, his voice sounding more echoey now.

"It appears that things have rapidly gone south and might be about to wrap up a lot quicker than I intended, thanks to Shaw." Marcus said through gritted teeth, but loud enough for his listeners to hear.

There was an audible gasp from the phone, more than likely from Alex.

"I wouldn't worry too much. I doubt they know you're involved, unless Shaw has turned you all in as well. But there is one last thing I need you guys to do. It may risk you being caught but if you're discreet you might just get away with it. Oakley, that large sack of Devils Breath I gave you, share it out between you four."

"Sure thing." Oakley answered back.

Once Oakley had confirmed that it all had been shared out, Marcus told them all what to do.

"Are you fucking serious!?" someone shouted down the phone.

"Absolutely. Fuck it."

There was an inaudible conversation that Marcus couldn't quite make out. Then Oakley, reluctantly, spoke down the phone. "We'll do it." Then there was a murmur of agreement.

Marcus smiled, "Good."

"What about you? What you gonna do?"

Marcus looked at the gun in his other hand, then towards the door. "There is one thing I need to take care of. Then, I'm gonna to lay low. Probably go to Colombia." He said, smiling at the thought.

There was a pause on the phone, then. "Good luck, Marcus."

Marcus hung up and threw the phone on the table.

CHAPTER 28

James had managed to pull the pipe away just enough to free the handcuff.

He considered for a moment waiting for Marcus, to pretend that he was still secured to the pipe, to wait for the right moment then surprise Marcus and fight his way out. But no sooner had the thought struck him, he heard the commotion again. He had to know what was going on. He carefully opened the door, walked up the short corridor, through the other door and snuck out into the large corridor. Dusk was beginning to fall, which made the corridor even more eerie. James had no idea where to go from here. Then he heard shouting coming from the door closest to him on his right. He crept up close to hear what the shouting was about, but he quickly surmised that it was in Spanish. *SHIT!* Foreign languages where never his strongest point. Then he heard Marcus yell. A second later there was a gunshot, followed by two more shots. James knew he had to intervene, but without his gun, which he assumed Marcus had taken off him along with his phone, he was helpless. He couldn't take Marcus on unarmed, not when Marcus had a gun. He would be as good as dead. Then he heard more talking, then another gunshot. James stood still, crouched down beside the door, breathing quietly. There was silence. Then Marcus started talking. Detective Cross quickly realised he was on the phone to his accomplices. He leant closer, listening intently to the phone call.

When Marcus had ended his conversation, James knew, in a matter of minutes, that Marcus would go back to the room to kill him. He quickly decided what to do.

Marcus walked out of the makeshift lab and out into the empty corridor. Gun in hand, he walked to the room where he had left James.

This ends now.

He pushed open the door to the room and walked in.

"Sorry about tha-" he halted when he saw that James wasn't there.

James swung the wooden stool as fast and hard as he could at the back of Marcus' head. James had snuck in, grabbed it and hid out of sight before Marcus had walked out of the makeshift lab. It was the only form of weapon that he could find. He swung it that hard that, upon impact, the stool broke into several pieces. Marcus fell to the dirty floor, in pain and momentarily dazed. James kicked as hard as he could onto Marcus' back.

"You motherfucker!" James screamed as he delivered the kicks. The professional side of Detective James Cross would- *should*- have secured and apprehended Marcus whilst he was incapacitated, but the way James now felt, Marcus had to pay, *really* pay, for his crimes. For killing Kelly and his baby.

Marcus tried in vain to get up during the attack, but James kept kicking him down. It was then Marcus saw the gun that he had dropped when James had hit him with the stool, just across from him on the floor. James was that focused on vengeance he hadn't even thought about the gun. Marcus, painfully, crawled over on all fours, all the while being kicked anywhere and everywhere on his body. James had shown no signs of relenting his attack. When James swung his foot back for another kick, Marcus lunged for the gun and grabbed it. He fell down and swung it upwards, pointing it and firing at James head, missing by inches, creating a smoking bullet hole in the ceiling.

Shit! James rushed through the open door into the corridor. He ran through the first door he saw, into the makeshift lab, and slammed the door.

Marcus struggled to his feet and ran after James. He stood alone in the corridor, listening for a noise. He should've killed James when he had the chance, but like a cat playing with a mouse before it went for the kill, he was having too much fun toying with him. He couldn't resist it.

Marcus approached the lab door, he knew he hadn't locked it, seeing as the chemists were all now dead, there was no point. He raised the gun in his hand and pushed the door with his other. As he was stepping through James ran, and slammed the door as hard as he could from the other side. Marcus fell backwards, dropping the gun. James opened the door and ran at him to kick him again, but Marcus had regained his balance and was too quick this time, and he landed a punch into James stomach, winding him. James fell over and Marcus kneed him in the face, breaking his nose and instantly causing blood to spurt out his nose over his mouth. Marcus stamped on his stomach, winding him even more. Then he stamped on James' ankle, breaking it, causing him to scream through a mouthful of blood.

James was curled on the floor, dazed and disorientated from the broken and bloody nose and trying to catch his breath, blood pouring from his nose and into his mouth. Marcus bent over and picked up the gun again. He stood above James and pointed the gun at him, panting heavily. "I had lost everything. Everything I ever loved. The world just carried on while mine was ending. I had enough. I wanted to take control."

James, still doubled over on the floor, scowled furiously. "Y-YOU TOOK EVERYTHING FROM ME! I DIDN'T LOSE IT! YOU TOOK IT! I WAS GOING TO BE A DAD! BUT THEY ARE DEAD NOW, BECAUSE OF YOU!" he spurted blood out of his mouth as he screamed.

"I told you, I never meant your wife to die. That was never my intention. I do, however, intend to kill you." Marcus pointed the gun at James's head and paused. "Fuck it," he said, throwing the gun down the corridor. He reached into his pocket and pulled out a small plastic bag. Tearing the top off carefully, he looked down at James.

"It seems kind of fitting that my last victim of *this*," he raised the bag above James. "is you." He then proceeded to tip the entire contents over James' face.

Once the bag was empty, Marcus dropped it to the floor next to James, who didn't move.

"Stand up, Detective Cross." Marcus said.

James laid still for a moment, before slowly pushing himself off from the floor and stood up awkwardly front of Marcus.

Neither men moved. Both were stood opposite each other, inches away. Marcus eventually started looking up and down at James.

"Detective Cross," Marcus said, stepping back and walked to the open lab door. "follow me." Marcus walked into the laboratory and James automatically followed, limping in. Both stepped over the chemist's dead bodies. Marcus stopped when he had gotten to the large metallic table that had the organised trays of drugs, measurement scales and cutting utensils on it. He picked up a scalpel and held it in front of him. James stopped and stood in front of Marcus with a vacant expression on his face.

"Hold out your hand," demanded Marcus. James done as he was told and held his right hand out. Marcus gave him the small knife.

"Now, cut your hand."

James turned the knife around in his hand and gripped the handle. He held open his left hand and he pressed the blade into it, just below his thumb and ran the blade across his palm. Blood oozed out as he pulled. There were no cries of pain. Just silence.

Marcus smiled widely as he watched James. He couldn't resist. He relished the effects of what this drug can do. It always made him feel like God.

After James had cut himself, Marcus took the scalpel from him and placed it back onto the table. James let his arms fall back down his side, blood dripping onto the floor from his left hand.

Smiling to himself, Marcus looked at James bloodied face. Then he frowned, as he saw a gold chain hanging around James' neck. He viciously grabbed the chain and pulled it up, dragging the pendant out of James' collar. "What's this shit?" Marcus said as he looked at the pendant and flipped it over, revealing the words on the back. He chuckled to himself as he read it. "Sounds like horseshit to me, but I'm pretty sure it meant something to you." Marcus said as he yanked the pendant around James' neck, breaking the chain. "Ooops, my bad!" he smiled cruelly at James blank expression, although he did notice that James' breathing had altered, and his eyes twitched when he pulled the chain off him. He wondered whether James was trying to fight it. He grinned evilly and shoved the pendant and broken chain into his pocket. Marcus looked at the table next to them, at the rest of the cutting utensils.

He saw a small machete next to the drug tray that contained the finished product.

That should be upstairs Marcus thought, smirking to himself as he saw it. *Enough is enough. Time to finish this.*

"James, pick up that machete, and slit your throat." Marcus sadistically said.

James slowly leant across the table to pick up the large knife with his right hand, and pressed the blade against his throat.

Marcus couldn't contain himself and laughed hysterically. He clenched his eyes shut as he laughed at the situation.

James took the momentary distraction and thrust the machete into Marcus' stomach, Marcus couldn't even scream at the unexpected agony. James quickly leant and grabbed the tray in the middle of the row and threw the contents over Marcus, who looked briefly terrified before his expression fell to a vacant look. James flung himself back onto the floor, landing on one of the dead chemists' bodies.

"Guess your shit don't work when the person can't breathe it in." James finally said, clutching his damaged hand close to his chest.

Before Marcus had tipped the Devils Breath over him, James had inhaled deeply though his bloodied mouth. He couldn't breathe though his broken nose. When Marcus had turned his back to him James, had tried to shake as much of the Devils Breath off as he could before quickly letting out a much-needed breath.

Detective Cross struggled to his feet and looked around the room. He saw a pile of paper towels on the other side of the room. Stumbling over, he grabbed a handful and wrapped some around his bleeding hand. Marcus, hunched over, gazed ahead expressionless. He began wavering on his feet as the small machete stuck out of his stomach, bleeding profusely. James limped back around and stood in front of him.

James considered his next move. Marcus was going to bleed to death either way, but he could prolong the inevitable by calling for help and stem the bleeding till help came, as pointless as it seemed.

But then he thought about Kelly and his unborn child.

"Marcus, slit your own goddamn throat."

Detective James turned, picked up Marcus' phone off the table and walked out the room. Marcus yanked the machete out of his stomach, causing more blood to spill out, and brought the blade up to his throat.

James pressed the side button on the phone and luckily it came to life. He dialled the number for Captain Fisher.

Captain Fisher was utterly shocked to hear from him. He had been presumed dead and half the city cops were searching for him. James gave Captain Fisher the location Marcus had told him and the whole place would be overrun with cops within 10 minutes. Detective Cross also told Captain Fisher of the phone call that Marcus had made.

"Christ Almighty! Okay James, leave it with me. Hold tight, son. Help is coming." Captain Fisher said before hanging up.

James turned and walked back into the lab. He stepped over the chemist's bodies and walked towards the table. On the floor next to it was Marcus, lifelessly gazing at the ceiling, glassy eyed. In his hand was the machete. His throat had been slit, and the fountain of blood from his throat had slowed down to a small jet spurting slowly. Blood also seeped onto the floor around his stomach. James leant down and fished his pendant and broken chain out from Marcus' pocket.

CHAPTER 29

Night had now fallen. St. Mary's hospital was swarming with nearly every cop in San Francisco. Two police helicopters circled noisily overhead, beaming intense searchlights around the vicinity of the hospital. Every corridor had at least five-armed officers bursting into every room uninvited, looking for Marcus' accomplices. All the doctors, nurses and patients were either upset, scared or even angry at sudden intrusion of the police force.

Martin King, the managing director of the hospital, burst out of his office and marched up to Captain Fisher, who was stood at the entrance of the hospital.

"Yes. OK. Keep circling till I inform you otherwise." Captain Fisher said, speaking into the police radio, communicating with the helicopters above.

"What the hell is going on here?!" Martin shouted, red faced.

Captain Fisher finished with the radio and clipped it onto his belt.

"And who are you?" Captain Fisher asked hastily.

"I'm the managing director of this hospital! I run this place! The staff and my patients are MY responsibility! Now please, tell me what the hell is going on here!" Martin demanded, frustratedly.

Captain Fisher looked apologetically at the man. "I

am sorry for this, but we have reason to believe that some people are on their way here now to this hospital intent on harming your staff and patients."

Martin frowned. "What the hell are you talking about?" he asked.

Captain Fisher took a deep breath and proceeded to tell him about a substance that can make even the nicest people do the most awful things, and that there were some people following orders to use it on the hospital staff.

Martin looked mortified, the colour drained from his face. "Good God... Does anything like that really exist? I-I have never heard of it. Who would make something like this? Who would *order* someone to do this?" he asked, shaking his head with every question.

"I'm afraid so," captain Fisher replied, "and as for *who* made it and ordered these people to come here... well, he has – sorry, had – some serious issues with the way you run this hospital."

A helicopter noisily flown by overhead. Jackson, Oakley, Sky and Alex squatted down as close to the wall as possible, out of view of the helicopters.

"SHIT!" Jackson yelled, narrowly ducking out the way of one of the helicopters searchlights. They were crouched down, hiding behind a building, lined up against a wall down the road from the hospital, which was no further than 400 yards away. They were following Marcus' orders; to go to St. Marys hospital and to use it on the hospital staff to kill the patients.

"What're they doing here?! They know we're coming! Marcus has been caught! He must've been! That's the only way they'd know about us!" Alex whispered, panicking.

A helicopter circled by again. Jackson glanced around the corner, looking for anyone approaching. He looked back at the others and shook his head. "We can't stay here. We gotta leave."

"I know a place. Not too far from here. We can lie low there for a while." Oakley suggested, at the back of the line.

They all nodded in agreement, checking that the coast was clear and ran through the side streets in the opposite direction.

Running into a small building just outside of "The Tenderloin", Oakley held the door open as they ran through.

"The room on the left." he said as he closed the door.

"They knew! They *Knew!*" Jackson said, waving his hands around, standing in the middle of the dark room. The only form of light was from their cell phones.

Sky and Alex were sat individually on some dusty wooden boxes near the walls, Alex on one side and Sky on the other. They both nodded in agreement as Jackson spoke.

Oakley walked in and closed the door. "Calm down, Jackson."

Jackson looked exasperated, "Calm down? Calm down?! They were there for *us!*" he said furiously. "And the only way they'd know about us is Marcus! He *must* have ratted us out!"

"I won't say it again. Calm down and shut up." Oakley replied. "This building is supposed to be empty. Any noise and people might get suspicious and, seeing as the police were there for us, this might *look* suspicious. Gettit?" he aggressively through gritted teeth.

Jackson immediately went quiet and looked worried. "Shit!" he whispered.

"What are we gonna do? We can't stay here forever!" Sky asked, worriedly.

"Listen," Oakley started saying. "We'll stay here for a few more hours then leave one by one, like we did before when Marcus wanted us to meet up. Okay?"

Jackson, Sky and Alex looked at each other and nodded.

"I don't know why the police were at the hospital, and I don't know what's happened to Marcus. But like he said, the police don't know who we are. They would've found us by now." Oakley said, addressing the room. "And as for Marcus, fuck him, I don't know about you guys, but I never really liked him much anyway. He didn't use the Devils Breath on us, but he may as well have. Ordering us about and shit. He just used us as pawns. I'm gonna take my share of Devils Breath and use it how *I* want to use it. Not how he wanted me to."

Jackson, Sky and Alex slowly smiled in unison, clearly inspired by Oakley's words.

"Yeah!" Jackson said, just louder than a whisper. "Fuck Marcus!"

Sky and Alex started laughing. "Yeah!" they said at the same time.

Oakley laughed. "This calls for a celebration!" he declared, heading out of the room.

Sky turned to Alex. "I still haven't even used what Marcus gave me before! I don't know who to use it on. Have you used yours?" she asked quizzically.

Alex suddenly looked alarmed, and hesitated before answering. "Umm, yeah I have. It was on some woman I bumped into."

Sky looked excited. "And? How was it?"

Alex started fiddling her fingers nervously, "It was good. Really good. It really does work."

Jackson chimed in. "I ain't used mine either. My folks have a load of money stashed away somewhere in their house, but I don't know where. I ain't seen them for years." He smiled menacingly. "I might just pay them a visit soon. Have a nice family reunion." He grinned nastily.

Oakley walked through the door carrying a small tray. He went to Sky first and bent down to her and offered her a spliff. She smiled like a child, gladly taking one and placing it in her lips.

"Don't light it just yet." Oakley said, smiling. "We're gonna have a toast!"

"No problem!" Sky said through pursed lips, spliff hanging from her mouth.

Oakley then went to Alex, and then Jackson, who both gladly took one. Oakley then took one himself and placed the empty tray on a box near him. He then raised the spliff in the air. "Cheers!" he said loudly. The others followed, stood in a circle and all tapped the tip of the spliff together "Cheers!" they all said, smiling and placing them in the mouths.

Oakley started patting his pockets. "Shit. I can't find my lighter."

"No worries man, you can use mine." Jackson said as he dug into his pocket and fished out his.

"Nah, man. It's my lucky lighter. I only ever use that one." Oakley replied, walking out of the room.

Jackson lit his and then passed the lighter to Alex, who passed onto Sky after lighting. They all inhaled, savouring the taste.

Oakley walked in a minute later wearing a face mask. Sky, Alex and Jackson were still stood up, silent and expressionless. Their arms had fallen down to their side and the devils-breath-laced spliffs were on the floor, slowly burning away.

"Sorry guys," Oakley said, his voice muffled through the mask. "But that Devils Breath is all mine." He reached into his pocket and pulled out a gun. He pointed it at Sky's head and pulled the trigger. Her body fell to the side. He then swung his arm to Jackson and shot him in the head. Then he pointed the gun at Alex's face and killed her.

Oakley didn't see the face in the window, watching him.

Oakley put the gun in his pocket and picked up the duffel bag containing the rest of the Devils Breath, stepped over the dead bodies and walked out of the room, into the dark hallway.

"FREEZE!" a cop had burst through the main door and stood in the hallway, torch and gun pointed at Oakley. Oakley jumped in shock and raised his hands.

"I saw you kill those people! I saw you all near the hospital. I followed you here, then you killed them!" the cop shouted.

Oakley had the gun in his left pocket and a bag of Devils Breath in his right pocket. He quickly went to grab them both.

The cop didn't hesitate to shoot him dead.

EPILOGUE

After the police had picked up James and the dead bodies from the building, a large room was discovered on the top floor. It contained 300 Jimson Weed plants which had scopolamine growing in the early stages before they bloomed. There was a huge glass ceiling and 30 high standing heaters were also in the room, essentially turning it into a greenhouse. How Marcus had obtained such a vast amount of plants and harvested the scopolamine still baffled the SFPD weeks later. Even the DEA couldn't help. All the plants were destroyed following the incident.

James Cross limped into Morrington Cemetery holding two large bouquets of flowers.
Following the incident, he attended counselling at Captain Fishers request, and they had advised him to take a few weeks off to "face his inner demons."
James walked up to Kelly's grave and placed down a bouquet.
His eyes were misty as he spoke. "I miss you so much, Kelly. I'm sorry I couldn't save you both. I love you Kacie." He sighed.
James stood soundlessly gazing at the grave, reminiscing about everything. After 10 minutes had passed, he

sighed. "See you again next week Kelly."

He then turned and headed further into the cemetery.

He stood in front of two graves that were together. He had found out that Sean Conner and Jennifer Reilly were buried next to each other, three days after Kelly's burial. He bent down and placed the bouquet between the two graves.

"I'm sorry you both had to go through what you did," James sighed.

"I forgive you."

THE END

Printed in Great Britain
by Amazon

33073808R10102